THE 79 SQUARES

THE 79 SQUARES

SQUARES.

Malcolm J. Bosse

THOMAS Y. CROWELL   NEW YORK

For Malcolm-Scott,
my best friend.

Copyright © 1979 by Malcolm J. Bosse
All rights reserved. Printed in the United States of America.
No part of this book may be used or reproduced in any manner
whatsoever without written permission except in the case of
brief quotations embodied in critical articles and reviews.
For information address Thomas Y. Crowell, 10 East 53 Street,
New York, N. Y. 10022. Published simultaneously in Canada by
Fitzhenry & Whiteside Limited, Toronto.
Designed by Harriett Barton

Library of Congress Cataloging in Publication Data

Bosse, Malcolm J   1926–
The 79 squares.
Summary: To the bafflement of his parents, gang, and
probation officer, visiting an ostracized, cantankerous
old man and his garden becomes very important to 14-year-
old Eric
    [1. Friendship—Fiction.   2. Old age—Fiction
3. Gardens—Fiction]   I. Title.
PZ7.B6494Se   [Fic]   79-7591
ISBN 0-690-03999-9   ISBN 0-690-04000-8 lib. bdg.
10 9 8 7 6 5 4 3 2 1

Contents

The Garden

The four boys waved at him from their booth and called out, "Hey there, Solo!"

Solo was the name they gave him, and that was how Eric knew he belonged to the gang. They didn't have an initiation; for that matter, they didn't call themselves "the gang." Their bond was their refusal to join any team or society or organization at school. The only sign of their exclusiveness was their special names: Zap, Horse, Superkool, and Bones. Having alienated themselves from everyone else, they demanded strict loyalty from one another. Who belonged to the gang belonged to nothing else.

Eric, like them, had dropped out of school activities in the past year. Now, with the school term ended and summer vacation begun, every day the gang got together, usually at Larry's for burgers and Cokes. Being outsiders, they counted heavily on staying together, and so were jealous of one another's time. If someone missed a day at Larry's, the others would ask the following day, "Where were you? Where?"

Solo never missed a day, aware that the gang was still testing his loyalty. He was especially worried about the impression he made on Superkool, who commanded more respect than Horse did, although Horse was a head taller. Superkool was a muscular boy with long blond hair who had a way about him that people took seriously. He carried a knife and boasted that he would cut anybody who messed with him. He had never hurt anyone, however, and Horse accused him of looking at too much television, but no one had tried to take his knife away.

As Solo took a seat beside the muscular boy, the rest of the guys got up to go to the bowling alley. Solo waited for Superkool to give the signal for the two of them to follow. Superkool sat there drinking a Coke, looking thoughtful. Then he turned with a faint smile and asked Solo if he'd like to smoke a little pot. The idea frightened Solo, who had never smoked it before, but there was no question of refusing. He agreed instantly and soon was walking with Superkool through a series of lawns and gullies.

As they hiked along, Superkool described this college guy who sold pot when he had more than he needed for himself. He was one of the few college guys who would sell to kids, so he was known. The thing was, they had to be careful. They strolled along the sidewalk across the street from the house and whistled. This college guy knew the signal, and if he was home, he'd come out and meet them at the corner. For fear of revealing his innocence, Solo muttered, "Yeah, I get you," and followed along.

The boys climbed out of a gully into a sunlit garden and halted abruptly when they saw near a gray clapboard house an old man sitting in a lawn chair. At first they were not sure he was awake. He sat motionlessly, his bony hands limp over the arms of the chair. Although it was a warm June day, he had a shawl wrapped around his neck. Tufts of white hair stood out on the sides of an otherwise bald head that shone like weathered parchment. What struck the boys, when they stepped closer, was the pair of intense eyes staring at them. Blue eyes, as blue as the sky itself. Then a thin hand raised from the chair arm and waved at them to approach. The wrinkled old face broke into a smile, but not a friendly one.

"Don't you ask permission," he said in a voice of surprising power, "when you track through a garden?"

Fixed by that voice, neither boy moved or spoke.

"I'm asking you, Don't you ask permission when you track through somebody's garden? You. I'm talking to *you.*" He pointed a gnarled finger at Solo.

Solo looked at his companion and shrugged.

"Is my question funny or something?" the old man persisted.

"We didn't even know you were here," said Solo.

The old man pursed his lips thoughtfully, then sat back in his chair. "Okay," he said. "What's your name?"

"You can call me Solo. Why not?"

"And yours?"

"What's it to you?" snapped Superkool.

The old man chuckled. "Manners haven't improved in the last forty years. I'll ask again, politely, *What is your name?*"

"What's yours?"

"Mr. Beck. And thank you kindly for asking."

The boys glanced in confusion at each other, then at the old man, who was grinning broadly.

"I had almost forgotten there were boys in the world,"
he said. "Or how to figure their ages. You, for example"
—he pointed again at Solo—"I figure you must be twelve."

Hurt, Solo replied, "I'm almost fourteen."

"You see? I have lost the ability to judge age," said the
old man with a mirthless laugh.

Again the boys glanced at each other.

"Now tell me your real name, Solo," the old man said
suddenly.

Solo just stared at him.

Mister Beck smiled. "Excellent manners, excellent." He
leaned forward to study the boys. "Spoiled kids haven't
changed much in the last forty years. Am I right? Not since
I last dealt with them. Things come and go, but spoiled kids
go on forever. Right? Am I right?" He rapped the arm of
the chair heartily.

The boys kept staring at the tanned head, the tar-
tan shawl, the outsized gray pants, and black shoes sticking out on the lawn as if unattached to a body that seemed
capable of blowing away, like a twig, in the first gust of
wind. The old man was all eyes and hands and malevolent
grin.

"Come on," murmured Superkool and gestured to Solo.
"Let's get out of here."

"You," shouted Mister Beck. "I bet you carry a knife.
Come on, deny it. I *dare* you."

Superkool's eyes widened. "How do you know that?"

"You damn fool. The outline of the handle's visible in
your right pants' pocket."

"I'm a boy scout."

Mister Beck laughed. "You? You're no boy scout."

"How do you know so much?"

"I look at people. I have developed the art of looking."

Both boys giggled and glanced at each other as if to say, This old guy is nuts.

"Come on," said Superkool and took a step across the lawn toward a fence.

"Wait," commanded Mister Beck. "Never carry a knife in that obvious manner. You let people know too much. I once knew a fella who understood a lot about knives, and he told me." The old man cleared his throat. "Go on, punk. You can go now."

Superkool studied the scowling face for a moment, then shrugged, and ambled away with his hands in his pockets. He yawned dramatically. "I'm going," he called to Solo before leaping the fence into the next yard.

"You, stay a minute," Mister Beck ordered Solo.

"Go ahead and stay," Superkool said with a laugh. "You know the address. I'll meet you there."

"He's right," said Mister Beck. "Stay a minute and see how nuts I am."

Laughing, Superkool vaulted the fence and disappeared.

For a moment Solo nearly followed his companion. After all, nothing kept him here except curiosity. Putting his hands on his hips, he glared defiantly at the old man.

"Come here, come on," coaxed Mister Beck. "I'm not nuts."

Solo hesitated, then walked slowly until he stood a few feet from the old man.

"Thank you," Mister Beck said in a gentle voice. "I just wanted to see someone that young up close again. I'm eighty-two years old."

Eighty-two. That made this old man seven years older than Solo's grandfather had been when he died. Solo had once thought that Grandfather was the oldest man in the world. Grandfather had fought in World War Two somewhere in Italy against the Germans.

"Were you in the war?" he asked Mister Beck.

"Which one? There's a choice, you know."

"World War Two."

"I was busy elsewhere during that war. I enlisted for World War One, but didn't get to France."

"World War *One?*"

"Never saw the Korean or Vietnam wars either. I just heard about them," Mister Beck said in a reflective tone, as if recalling his own life when those wars were being fought. Then abruptly he said, "Look at me."

The boy looked.

"With great care!"

"I am."

"Carefully!"

"I am," the boy claimed with impatience.

"Tell me what you see. *Exactly* what you see. No holds barred."

When tested in a strange way by adults, Solo had a pat reply: "I don't know."

"I know you don't know," said Mister Beck gruffly. He swept his arm through the bright air. "What is all this around you?"

The boy glanced around quickly. "A garden, I guess."

"That's right. That's the strict truth—you *guess.* You don't know for sure. You're looking but not seeing. But I could show you what's here," the old man declared. "I have been looking at things carefully for the last forty years, and I have developed a method."

Solo felt uneasy. He wanted to catch up with Superkool, even if it meant smoking pot for the first time. That would be better than listening to this crazy old man. Yet Solo did not move one step; he was trapped by those intense blue eyes.

"Well?" said Mister Beck. "What about it? Have you got the stuff to try? Do you want to see this garden?" The old man grinned in the silence. "Think I'm nuts? I'll tell you something. You are the one who's nuts if you don't come back here tomorrow and start *looking at this garden!*"

Solo said nothing, but ambled away as casually as possible, leaving the garden the way he had entered it—through the gully. At the edge of the lawn, he paused and turned and muttered over his shoulder, "The name's Eric."

☿ ☿ ☿

He awoke the next morning with sunlight streaming across his bare chest. Blinking rapidly, he tried to remember a dream, but it got away from him. He glanced at the other bed, relieved to see that his young brother had already gone. Roddy was nine—old enough to be a nuisance, too young to be a companion. Eric wanted his own room and would have had it but for the window-breaking episode. That had cost him privacy.

He heard sounds outside the window. A car was backing out of the driveway; the wild sputter suggested it was the Porsche and Mother was backing out recklessly as usual. He lay on the bed and waited until he heard the deep drone of the Cadillac moving more cautiously into the street: Father, this time. Eric glanced at the watch that he had earned last year by getting a good grade in math. In a couple of minutes his sister would be hurrying to her summer job at McDonald's. He waited until the door slammed: Susan was gone. Roddy must be halfway to the ball park. So the whole family was finally out of the house. Since the window-breaking episode, Eric had avoided them as much as possible.

That episode had occurred near the end of the school year. Leaving Larry's he and Bones had sped off on their bikes, grim and furious, without anything in mind, but filled with the need to express their frustrations about school and the future. They rode until they were there, gazing up in the dusk at the windows of their junior high school, from which they would soon be graduated. They had been betrayed, used, cheated. They had come without exchanging a word, like iron filings drawn to a magnet.

"Let's go," said Eric.

"Where?" asked Bones.

"To get ammunition."

They sped off again, stopping this time at an abandoned rock quarry. Long past their dinner hour they returned to the school with their bike baskets heavy with rocks. Working with cool deliberation, they piled the rocks in front of the school building.

Giggling, Bones looked up at the moonlit windows and said, "Are we really going to?"

For an answer Eric threw the first rock. The pane of glass shattering was like shattering his memory of one school and his anticipation of another. With zest and conviction, he threw a second rock, putting into this throw the full weight of frustrations both real and imagined. Bones took aim, too, and heaved a rock. Then they were raining stones against the building. So intent were they that they failed to see the flashing light of the car moving down the street. By the time they heard "Stay where you are!" it was too late.

Hauled down to the police station, they readily confessed, although neither could explain the reason for their vandalism to police or parents. Because it was their first offense, they received six months' probation.

Less than a week after this adventure, the gang had called him by his new name, Solo. He figured they had given him the name because of his lonely ways, but of course he never asked for an explanation. He was new in the gang. In a sense he was on two probations: one with the police and one with them.

Alone in the house now, he could get up, go downstairs, and make his own breakfast. He took the stairs three at a time, belching assertively by swallowing air. Plates and glasses filled the table in the breakfast nook, awaiting the housekeeper who came every day now that Mother served on so many committees and was rarely home.

Eric made some toast and warmed up the coffee that Mother had left for him on the stove. It was tacitly agreed by the family that he could eat alone. The thing was, he liked to have his breakfast alone. It enabled him to watch soap operas on the kitchen television, something his mother would not have allowed had she been there. He enjoyed soap operas because life in them was livelier than in Forest Park.

He ate five slices of toast, smeared with jam and butter, and drank three cups of coffee, but no orange juice, as his mother always wanted him to drink it. On the Sony he watched Laura Miles tell Dr. Michael Rollins that her dead baby was not her own but in fact was the offspring of Grace

Andrews, who had been having an affair with Richard, Laura's husband, so they must face the problem squarely. Richard came into the room just as Dr. Rollins, in an effort to console her, had put his arm around Laura's shoulder. The program ended with the trio frozen in attitudes of anger, surprise, and fear, so Eric turned off the set and wandered about the house. He found himself upstairs, passing Susan's room. There was no sense in trying her door, because she always kept it locked. Not that there was anything in it worth looking at. He strolled into his room, glancing at Roddy's toys and his own model airplanes, which he had not touched in a year and which he would not let Roddy touch until his little brother was a year older. Eric yawned. He looked out the open window at the neighborhood. There were always delivery trucks with visor-capped men carrying packages into one house or another. It was an expensive neighborhood. Eric glanced at his watch, for it was necessary to leave the house before the housekeeper arrived; she was a nice lady but talked too much. Again he trudged downstairs and stared a moment at the television, tempted to watch another soap opera, which he would have done had there been a soap opera at that time of morning. There was only a game show available—and a program for toddlers. It wouldn't have been the first time he had watched the program for toddlers, something he never admitted to anyone, hardly even to himself.

Sipping a cold cup of coffee, he tried to plan his day prior to meeting the gang at Larry's. He could bike over to Superkool's house, but he was not welcome there. Five times this summer he had gone there, but Mrs. Lindblum always told him that her son was not at home, even though

Superkool had waved at him from the window. Superkool might carry a knife and smoke pot, but he was not allowed to have inside his house a friend on police probation.

Eric wondered about yesterday. After he had left the strange old man in the garden, he had dutifully sought out Superkool at the college guy's house. Eric had found the right address, but no Superkool. He had prowled the neighborhood for half an hour without luck. Maybe the college kid had waved Superkool away, but at least Superkool might have waited nearby. From anyone else Eric would have demanded an explanation for being left in the lurch, but he dared not ask Superkool.

Eric left the house and went into the garage that opened and shut on electronic signal. Father was excited by any gadget with a button to press that made something happen. Father's favorite gadget at the moment was the garage signal. Eric examined his bike, fiddled with the gears, and kicked the spokes to make sure they were okay. Some guys knew all about bikes. Zap, for example. That guy could spot a bike three blocks away and tell you the make, model, gearing system, and retail price at the local bicycle store. Eric kicked a tire lazily and drew a deep sigh. What he might do before Larry's opened, he might take a little hike. So he crossed the back lawn and began the steep descent into a gully. Excluding the business district, he could walk across the whole town just by following the ravines. He had gone through a number of them before realizing where he was going. He surprised himself. He had never meant to see that garden again and the crazy old man who sat in it. But that was what he was going to do. And as he climbed up the gully, he recalled the dream that had eluded him this morning. In the dream he had seen the old man, who had been laughing and telling him something in a foreign language. Was he really going to see the old nut? Well, it would pass the time until Larry's opened and he could join the gang.

Eric trudged up the steep side of the gully and emerged into the garden.

꙰ ꙰ ꙰

The old man was sitting exactly where he had been yesterday, with the same shawl around the scrawny neck. Today, beside him on a table, there were a pitcher and glasses—two glasses.

Eric turned to leave again when the old man called triumphantly, "You're right on time!"

Eric looked over his shoulder and saw Mister Beck waving at him to come back into the garden.

"Right on time!"

"Never said I was coming," Eric mumbled, but came back into the garden.

"No, you didn't, but you're on time anyway."

Eric took a few steps and halted.

"Come on. I'm not nuts."

Eric smiled faintly and walked across the lawn, stopping near the seated man.

"I'd offer you some lemonade, but you haven't worked for it yet. In this garden you don't get something for nothing."

"Never said I wanted anything."

"You'll want the lemonade after you work."

"Work? Never said I'd work." Eric scuffed his shoes in the grass, thinking the whole thing was crazy.

"What are you looking at?" the old man asked abruptly.

"Nothing. At my shoes, I guess."

"That's too bad."

Eric looked at the frowning old face. "What is?"

"That you're not looking at anything but your shoes. There's so much to see!"

Eric didn't know how to react to such passion in an old man.

"Tell me what you see right now," said Mister Beck. "This moment."

"A garden."

"A garden? What's a garden? Tell me what you *see*!"

"Well, I—don't know."

"If you want to leave," Mister Beck said coldly, "then leave."

"I mean it. I don't know."

"So look around." Mister Beck added, "Just for the hell of it."

Eric liked the spirit of that last remark, and he gave the garden a real appraisal. "Okay," he said after a few minutes, "I looked."

"Tell me exactly."

"I see the house."

"You mean the back of the house. East side."

"Well, sure," Eric muttered, about ready once again to take off. Yet he remained there, held by the powerful voice and the intense blue eyes.

"Tell me exactly what you see, beginning at the northeast corner."

Eric stared at the trellis against the side of the small garage. "Flowers."

"What kind?"

"I don't know."

"Morning glories. They close in another hour." Mister Beck gestured impatiently. "Go on. What's next?"

Eric haltingly but methodically described the rest of the garden—flower bed, tree, bush, fence, the next flower bed, tree, and bush. Finished at last, he stood with hands on hips. The garden seemed bigger than it had been before he started to enumerate everything in it.

"Done?" asked Mister Beck; and when Eric nodded, he said with a laugh, "You forgot something."

Eric glanced quickly around, sure he had mentioned everything.

"The birdbath!" Mister Beck observed sharply.

"Yes, well, that."

"Yes, well, that," Mister Beck repeated sarcastically. "Now shall we start?"

"Start what?"

"Why, what we discussed yesterday. You looking at this garden."

"I just did."

Mister Beck reached out and shakily picked up something from the table. He tossed it at Eric, who caught the thing in midair. It was a measuring tape housed in a steel container. "Measure the garden."

"What?"

"I said, Measure the garden. Take every dimension. Measure the size of each flower bed, each tree. Measure the height of the trellis. Measure the circumference of the birdbath. Measure everything except ourselves." Mister Beck pointed to a small notebook lying on the table. "Record every dimension."

Eric met the intense blue eyes until his own gaze wavered and broke contact. "All right," he said.

Mister Beck then told him to anchor the tape in the ground by cutting some pegs from a tree in the ravine. He pointed to a kitchen knife also lying on the table.

Without a word, Eric took the knife and scrambled into the gully, looking for low branches. He took hold of one, lifted the knife, and paused. What was he doing? Measuring a stupid garden for a crazy old man? What did the old man want? And why, when the old man told him to do something, did he do it? But the questions stopped when he cut through the branch. Soon he had whittled some pegs and returned to the garden.

For the next hour he reeled out the tape, anchored it in the ground, and took dimensions. Never in his life had he measured anything with such care, but then never had such fierce eyes been watching him. When he had measured a side of the garden, he was told by the old man to measure again, and then again, to make sure it was accurate. After three measurements Mister Beck would nod his approval. "Good," he'd say. "Taking the average of the three measurements, we arrive at thirty-five feet, seven-and-one-quarter inches for the west side of the garden." The way Mister Beck pronounced the measurement, it was like an Olympic record.

"Continue," said Mister Beck, and Eric did throughout the morning. He drew a little map in the notebook and listed the calculations. It was kind of goofy, but the work passed the time. Mister Beck finally offered him a glass of lemonade. The old man looked like a baggy suit stuffed with straw, but he was no fool. Eric smiled at him; the old man smiled back. Ice had melted in the pitcher long ago, but the lemonade was still cool. Eric drank his without pausing. He glanced down at his perspiration-soaked T-shirt; it clung to his chest.

"Lemonade good?" asked Mister Beck, who only sipped his.

Eric nodded.

"Have another glass." While Eric poured it, the old man sighed. "When I was very young, I went to sea. Forgotten most of what happened—whole years of it—but I still remember a particular drink of water I had after working hard in the hot sun."

Eric waited for more reminiscences, because talking about the past was something he expected old people to do. Grandfather had talked endlessly about the past. But Mister Beck stopped right there. Although Eric was curious about the old man, he was glad that Mister Beck had stopped. Eric found it difficult to listen when old people talked about their adventures. He couldn't imagine them, all wrinkled and feeble, doing the energetic things they claimed to have done. And so he was relieved that Mister Beck sent him back to work, completing the measurements. Finished at last, Eric wiped the sweat from his eyes and stared with satisfaction at the little map in the notebook. He had made this map; it was his. But what was he supposed to do with it?

As if hearing this unspoken question, Mister Beck said, "You aren't finished, you know."

Eric looked up from the map.

"Did you think that was all there was to it?" Mister Beck asked, frowning. "Did you suppose you could simply measure the garden, and you would have it in your mind and heart?"

Eric hesitated, then replied boldly, "I didn't suppose anything."

"Good, I'm glad you didn't. And the truth is," Mister Beck said with a faint smile, "you made a beginning. You know something about this garden, its size, its design. But do you know what that's really like? That's like saying a man is five feet eight and weighs a hundred-fifty pounds. It says little about the person and certainly nothing about how he thinks or acts. It doesn't lay out his loves and hates and dreams." Mister Beck slapped the arm of his chair. "Enough for today. At eighty-two a man gets tired."

"Can I help you into the house?" Eric asked impulsively.

The blue eyes narrowed. "I can get there under my own steam, thank you."

Eric knew he had made a mistake; it wasn't easy dealing with a fierce old man. "Well, can I take the glasses and pitcher in?"

"My daughter will do that," Mister Beck said, "when she gets home from work."

Eric shrugged and glanced around during a long, awkward silence.

"See you tomorrow," the old man said finally.

Eric put the tape on the table and turned to leave.

"No, it's yours." Mister Beck was holding out the tape. "You'll be needing it," he said and tossed the tape to Eric.

For a moment Eric wondered if he should thank Mister

Beck, but there was a cold look in the old man's face that told him not to do it. Mister Beck simply wanted him to come back tomorrow and continue the work—whatever the work really was. They had gone somehow beyond differences in age into a strange kind of relationship, as if they were explorers who counted on each other for survival. Something like that. As Eric descended the gully, he had a flashing image of two men in fur jackets bracing into a chill wind in the desolate Arctic. Near the bottom of the slope, he heard the old man call after him, "Tomorrow! On time!"

❄ ❄ ❄

For dinner the Fischers had stew and salad. Mother had once taken classes in gourmet cooking, but she never had time to practice her skills, so the housekeeper prepared either stew or a casserole and shoved it during the day into the warming oven.

Eric bolted his food, having worked up a keen appetite in the garden. Finished, he laid his hands on either side of the plate and watched his sister eat. Susan had a tendency to gain weight, was always on a diet, and approached her dinner like a soldier entering combat—tense, alert, suspicious. She handled the fork nervously, searching for veins of fat which she removed before allowing herself to eat finicky pieces of meat. What the family didn't know was how hungry Susan would become later—although Eric knew. More often than not, she would sidle up to his door and poke her head into the room and with studied nonchalance ask him if he might spare a bit of candy. He kept candy bars in his desk just for her. In recent years they had rarely clashed, but they were wary of each other. He kept the candy as a kind of peace offering.

Roddy had also finished eating and was staring ahead at nothing. Eric marveled at his young brother's patience. Roddy rarely made a misstep with adults—he knew instinctively how to please them. There was a special understanding between Roddy and Father, based on their placid manners and regular habits. Father, for example, ate according to a definite plan with a steady rhythm. Meat first, vegetables next, and salad last. The procedure never varied.

On the other hand, Mother ate in fits and starts that were geared to her conversation. While she talked, her fork hovered unsteadily above the plate, then plunged recklessly into whatever food happened to be under it. Tonight she was talking about one of her numerous organizational jobs. Eric usually tuned out when this happened, but his ears pricked up at the word "elderly." The word made him think of Mister Beck. Mother was a volunteer for an agency that sponsored a club for senior citizens, and this morning she had gone to welcome a newcomer to Forest Park.

"Eighty-two years old," she announced.

Eric sat up.

"Yes," Father murmured in a tone that could mean either a statement or a question.

Mother went on to say that the old man's daughter had brought him to town sometime in the spring. The woman was Miss Beck—the name Beck had Eric sitting up even straighter—the person who ran that little gift shop on Cottage Lane.

"Yes," Father said, finishing the vegetables and turning his fork toward the salad, while Mother's fork remained poised in the air.

"I went to their house this morning," Mother continued, "and knocked on the door. This Miss Beck answered but wouldn't open the door more than a crack, even though I told her I wasn't selling anything. I identified myself, but she kept holding the door. And then from inside the house came this absolutely terrifying shout. I asked her, 'Is that your father?' But before she could answer, this absolutely powerful voice yelled, 'Get that woman the hell out of here!' "

Eric guffawed.

"You think it's funny?" Mother bristled. "What's so funny? I take the time to welcome an old man, and all he does is insult me. I don't call that a bit funny."

Eric felt all eyes on him. "Sorry," he muttered, "I was thinking about something else."

"If you think it's funny," Mother said testily, "it's perfectly all right with me. I'd just like you to explain the basis of the humor; that's all."

"I really was thinking of something else." And it was true. He had been thinking of a hypothetical scene in which his mother had marched into the garden to welcome the old man and Mister Beck had handed her a measuring tape.

Eric wanted to tell the family about today, but how could he explain it? He couldn't make sense of it. He couldn't say the eighty-two-year-old man, who had shouted Mother out of the house, had also gotten him to measure a garden. Since the window-breaking episode the family had regarded him with suspicion. Telling them about Mister Beck and the garden would hardly restore their confidence in him.

The smart thing to do would be to forget all about the old man.

❧ ❧ ❧

The next day Eric was there on time. Mister Beck seemed impatient to get started. He asked if mathematics was still taught in school, because Eric would need it in order to compute the area of the garden. The old man didn't explain why. Eric knew him well enough already to know that Mister Beck would explain it in his own good time and not before. Then Mister Beck shoved the notebook at Eric and demanded that the species of every flower and tree in the garden be labeled next to their locations on the map. If Eric couldn't identify everything, then he must get books and learn.

Eric bent over the map, feeling somewhat shaken by the authoritative tone that the old man had taken with him. That was the sort of thing he had disliked in school; now here he was during summer vacation taking orders from someone who wasn't even a teacher. And yet he understood the sense of Mister Beck's demand: If you were going to describe the garden, you might as well do it correctly. A flower was a rose or buttercup; a tree was an oak; and if you made a map that located them, you might as well include their names.

Eric took a deep breath of decision; he'd get the books. Glancing up to tell Mister Beck that he would, Eric was surprised by the wrinkled old face slumped against the thin chest. Mister Beck had fallen asleep—suddenly, like a baby.

For a moment Eric felt a twinge of contempt for the frail man in the chair, but then he remembered those blue eyes with a cold fire in them that could make him do crazy things like measure a garden.

And now he was going to calculate the area of the garden, although he hated math.

Leaving the old man snoring in the chair, Eric went straight home and set to work on the problem. He got out his math books and labored hard at it. At last he tossed the pencil aside. He had first worked the problem by figuring the area of a trapezoid—a quadrilateral with two parallel sides—that constituted the shape of the garden. Result: 2,856 square feet. He checked his solution by working the problem differently. He added the area of a rectangle and a triangle together: 2,856 square feet. He had the solution.

Larry's was open, and the gang was probably sitting in a booth by now, but Eric had something to do first before going there. He biked down to the public library and found *North American Trees* in the botany section. He looked up "pin oak" because it was one of the few trees he knew— there was a pin oak in the garden. He located the tree under *Quercus palustris.* The description contained words that he had never seen before: deciduous, obovate, glabrous, silvical, and others. He couldn't make sense of the description until he looked up at least a dozen words in the dictionary. So he did. Then he got a book on flowers and carried the two to the front desk. What was he doing? Here he was checking out scientific books on subjects that didn't really interest him, just so he could label stuff on a map. Just because an old man told him that he must. What would the gang think? What would Zap say? Zap had one eye that strayed, so he couldn't focus both of them at once on anything, and perhaps this made him dislike anything unusual or different. He made fun of people who did unusual things, and that would certainly include a guy who suddenly took an interest in flowers and trees. Then Horse would get into it. Horse was dead set against anything that excluded the gang.

Eric wanted to tell them about Mister Beck and the garden. He needed another slant on this thing, because measuring the garden and mapping it and calculating its area was a very strange thing for him to do. But he couldn't tell the gang and get away with it. Having friends did not mean you could trust them.

❊ ❊ ❊

Larry's was a large room with a front counter, some booths, and a juke box. Large plate-glass windows faced the street leading from the junior high. At any time of year the place was filled with kids. They never gave Larry trouble; he was a big muscular man who had once been a local football star. Parents considered it to be the safest place in town for their kids.

When Solo opened the screen door, he noticed Superkool sitting in a back booth. Solo waved, but Superkool merely waited for him with arms folded, lips tight.

"Where have you been?" he asked when Solo slid into the booth.

"Around," Solo replied vaguely.

"I mean yesterday. I can see where you've been today," said Superkool, pointing at the books that Solo was putting on the bench beside him.

"Yesterday? I had some work to do around the house. Where are the guys?"

"Bowling. Horse was wondering when you'd ever show up."

"Why aren't you bowling?" Solo asked, trying to change the subject.

Superkool lifted up his right hand, displaying a bandage. He giggled. "Cut myself with the damn knife."

The waitress came along with her order pad. Kids said that she had been working at Larry's before most of them were born. She sure wasn't young. Her red hair didn't seem to be her own, because it often changed shades, and sometimes patches of gray appeared at the roots. She was thin, bony, and wore enormous comfort shoes.

Solo ordered a Coke. She tapped the pad impatiently with her pencil. "And potato chips," he added, after which she flipped the pad shut.

"Let me see them."

Solo looked across the table at Superkool, who had his hand stretched out.

"Come on," said Superkool. "Let me see the books."

"Why?"

"Why not. Come on."

Reluctantly Solo picked them up from the bench and handed them over.

Superkool whistled, squinting at the titles. "Since when were you a nature lover?"

"Since a long time," Solo lied.

"Come on. What are the books for?"

"To read."

Superkool grinned unpleasantly. "So don't tell me. Who

cares?" he said, as a new record started on the juke box. He snapped his fingers to the rhythm. "I want to learn drums, but my dad says no. He says he wants a lawyer in the family, not a freak. Do you go for drums?"

"Sure."

"Horse won't believe it."

"I always liked drums."

"Believe it about you and nature." Superkool fingered the books speculatively. "Do you know that kid in seventh grade—Kenny Wilson? He keeps a bunch of snakes in the garage. Do you do stuff like that, too?"

Solo hooted contemptuously.

"Yeah, but you read these books."

"Nothing wrong with nature," Solo observed in a calm voice.

"Who said there was? Only you never told us you were into the birds and the flowers. It's just you never told us."

The Coke and potato chips came. Solo offered the open bag to his friend, who took half of them in one handful. Superkool had the fully developed arms of a grown man.

"How long did you stay with that old guy the other day?"

"Not long," replied Solo guardedly.

"Why did you stick around?"

"Just to see what he'd do."

"Well, what did he do?"

Solo took a long drink of his Coke; it gave him time to form an answer. Finally he replied. "He talked about the old days when he was a sailor."

Superkool nodded. "I have a grandfather like that. To hear him, you'd think he was the toughest guy who ever lived. Always remembering fights he had. But I guess he was pretty tough. I know he beat up my dad when my dad was our age." Superkool looked down at his open hands, as if judging them against the hands of his grandfather. "Last year he stayed with us a few weeks. He got mad at me and yanked off his belt. I told him, 'You hit me with that, old man, I'll kill you.' "

Solo stared at the girlishly long blond hair, at the cool blue expressionless eyes, at the thick forearms. "Did he tell your parents?"

"I don't think so." Superkool added with a sudden grin, "I think he was scared of me."

Solo felt uneasy. He often did around Superkool, who could abruptly change from a kid his own age into someone else, someone older, with a different way of looking at things.

"The other day," Solo said, "I tried to find you at that address."

Superkool cocked his head—he had forgotten that Solo had promised to meet him at the college boy's house. Superkool had a way of making you promise to meet him somewhere, then not showing up himself. It was something that made Horse furious.

"I mean the address of that college guy. You know—" Solo bent forward to say in a low voice, "The joint."

Superkool shrugged. "Oh, well, the guy wasn't home, so I left."

Solo picked up his books as unobtrusively as possible. He slid out of the booth.

"Don't you want that Coke?" Superkool asked.

"You finish it."

"See you tomorrow," said Superkool, pulling the glass in.

"If I can." Solo waved, turned, and started out of Larry's. "Sure you can," he heard at his back.

⁂ ⁂ ⁂

In following days Eric managed to see the gang, either at Larry's or the swimming pool or the bowling alley, but mornings he spent with Mister Beck in the garden. He spent hours with the books until finally he could identify all the plants in sight. He printed the names of every species alongside the spaces on the map. When that became torn and crowded, he brought a large sheet of paper from home, a ruler, and a pen, and copied out a better map. A week passed this way. Most of the time Mister Beck sat quietly in his chair, with the shawl around his neck, his bald head gleaming like polished wood in the sunlight, his blue eyes fixed at a spot in the air, his gnarled hands folded. But Eric knew that the old man was aware of everything that happened in the garden. For example, he pointed out to Eric a squirrel who stayed in the shagbark hickory. He had named it Roger. And when Eric was reading one of the books under a tree or printing a name on the map, he felt the old man's presence, those blue eyes burning into his back. But it wasn't a bad feeling. In fact, he felt a sense of well-being, knowing that Mister Beck, awake or dozing, was nearby. And yet he still didn't know what he was doing in the garden. Mister Beck had not explained the need for computing its area. All Mister Beck did in that week was glance now and then with approval at the map which was becoming increasingly complex. And he suggested that Eric should read books about wildlife and insects and birds. "It will be harder for you to identify the animal life. Plants stay put; animals don't." When Eric would stop for a glass of lemonade and look across the garden, he saw pin oak, shagbark hickory, sugar maple, and cottonwood; and in the flower beds in the brilliant sunlight there were marigolds, snapdragons, nasturtiums, asters, zinnias, roses, geraniums, dahlias, peonies, and sweet William. He looked at the bordering shrubs, the Amur privet and Japanese barberry. It was a wonder; he had all their names not only on the map but in his head.

Once when he was leaving the garden, Mister Beck stopped him with a smile and said, "You worked hard today. And I learned something about the garden myself."

"Did you?"

"Don't look so surprised. I didn't know the names of most of those flowers. I learned them from you." The old man leaned forward, squinting in the light. "Eric, do you think I'm lying?"

Eric shook his head, but without conviction.

"I am not condescending. You think I'm pretending not to know the names, just to make you feel important? Is that what you think?"

"Yes," Eric mumbled.

"Glad to get that out in the open. You see, I have a method for looking at this garden. These past forty years I learned about looking. But as for the garden, I don't know much, so I'm looking at it with no more knowledge than you have. That's the damn truth."

Eric met the steady blue eyes. "Okay," he said. "I believe you."

"Good. We understand each other. Now go home," the old man said. It was only after Eric was stumbling down the ravine that he realized Mister Beck's voice had been choked with emotion. The old man, Eric figured, must have been lonely a long time, sitting there all day with nothing to do and nowhere to go. Maybe Mister Beck had been lonely for the past forty years that he was always mentioning. He spoke of those years as if they were very special. They'd be special all right, if he had been lonely through all of them. But then Eric remembered that Mister Beck had a daughter, and that the daughter had been the one who planted and maintained the garden. It made Eric feel more comfortable to know that Mister Beck had this daughter to take care of him. Eric wondered what she was like—and soon had the opportunity to find out.

It was the next day after he and Mister Beck had shared a piece of steak. Mister Beck had told him to get it from the refrigerator, and so for the first time Eric entered the house. The small kitchen was immaculate; the steak had been wrapped in foil with the care of a gift package. From this alone, he knew that Miss Beck was an orderly person. While they ate the steak in the sunlit garden, Mister Beck in a voice of peculiar timidity asked Eric to drop by his daughter's store that afternoon. "Would you?" the old man said. "I think her phone's out of order. I'd like you to have her bring home a tin of chewing tobacco for me. I use it in the evening, watching television," he added.

Chewing tobacco. Eric was surprised that the stuff was still on the market. He thought it had gone out with the end of the nineteenth century. But come to think of it, Mister Beck had actually been *alive* in the nineteenth century. So after leaving the garden, but before meeting the gang at

Larry's, Eric rode his bike downtown to a side street called Cottage Lane where Miss Beck had her gift shop.

He leaned his bike against the wall and studied the front of the shop; it was small, the windows filled with bric-a-brac. Above the entrance was a white board with the painted red letters: THE LONELY HUNTER. Eric went in, hearing a bell tinkle over his head as he opened the door. There were two women in the shop, bending over a table on which a half-dozen dolls were standing. Eric glanced around; every possible bit of space had been used, yet so clean was the room that it didn't seem crowded. There were all sorts of things there: china plates, old bed warmers, ceramic ashtrays, trinkets in bowls, and better jewelry in glass cases. The stuff in general looked unusual, as if Miss Beck had gone to a lot of trouble finding something special. And he figured it must be expensive.

He was glad that a customer was there, so while he was waiting, he could have a good look at Mister Beck's daughter. Somehow the woman's relationship to the old man was important to Eric. She was rather tall and rawboned, with gunmetal-gray hair pulled back in a spinsterish bun. Her voice, speaking low to the customer, had a pleasant, almost musical quality to it. Her words were chosen carefully, and as she leaned forward, pointing out features of the doll dressed in a peasant costume, she emanated a spirit of calm. Eric liked her immediately. But when the customer had purchased a doll and left, and when Miss Beck turned to regard him, he saw an expression on her face that he didn't like.

"You must be Eric," she said flatly and stepped behind the counter, resting both hands proprietorially on the glass.

Eric nodded and gave Miss Beck the old man's request. Just at that moment the phone rang. While Miss Beck talked to someone, Eric remembered that Mister Beck thought the phone was out of order. But had the old man really thought so? It occurred to Eric that maybe the old man had wanted him to meet Miss Beck and so had arranged it this way. But why? It was no good trying to figure out the motives of old people.

When Miss Beck finished talking on the phone, she turned back to him with the same critical expression, the same stance of defensiveness at the counter. Plainly she did not like him.

"So you're Eric," she said and paused.

Their eyes met.

"I don't know what you're doing," Miss Beck said, "but please remember he's an old man."

Eric was startled. "What?" was all he could think of saying.

"My father tells me you stay in the garden with him. He's teaching you to look at it. I think I know what he means, but I wonder if you do."

"No," said Eric. "I don't think I do."

"Why do it then?"

"I don't know." Then he added, without thinking, "I like your father."

The woman studied him until Eric was about ready to turn and run out of there. "All right," she said in a low voice. "But you should know this. My father is a very unusual man; he has suffered terribly in his life; he's old and needs peace and quiet. I don't know why, but he trusts you. So, please, don't hurt him."

"Is that all?" Eric said coldly, feeling his fists clenched at his sides.

In a gentler voice Miss Beck said, "I'm sorry; I know I've angered you. But he believes in you, and I don't want him hurt."

"How could I hurt him?"

"By not believing in him as he believes in you."

Eric grunted in fury and exasperation. Did this woman think he would hit an old man or insult him? Eric was out on the street and pedaling his bike before he knew what he was doing.

As fast as he could pedal, he returned to the gully, chained his bike to a tree, and descended. Soon he was climbing up into the garden, then confronting the old man, who started out of a nap.

Eric did not beat around the bush. He told Mister Beck about the interview, about Miss Beck being suspicious of him, which was something he didn't understand and didn't like. She had no reason to talk to him like that; he hadn't done anything.

When Eric had finished his rushed little speech, Mister Beck sighed. "I'm glad that is over," he said. "You see, my daughter is very protective. Until a few months ago we hadn't seen much of each other for years, so now we're making up for lost time. She wants to take good care of me. Now in her mind—" Mister Beck's expression sharpened "—a boy your age might make fun of an old man like her father. But you and I know differently. That's why I wanted you to meet her. So now she knows, too."

Eric wasn't sure that he had convinced her of anything, but did not say so to Mister Beck. Instead he asked the old question, the one that Miss Beck herself had prompted him to consider again: "Mister Beck, what exactly does looking at the garden mean?"

"That's what we are going to find out."

"Miss Beck said you knew."

"Did she? Then she knows more than I do."

Eric realized it was no good asking more of the old man. So he asked another question prompted by his meeting with Miss Beck: What did the name of her store mean?

"A lot of people ask her," Mister Beck replied. "It comes from the title of a book: *The Heart Is a Lonely Hunter.* She says it means people search for love like hunters search for game. You see, Eric, my daughter is a very unusual woman."

It was the same phrase Miss Beck had used to describe him.

"I'll get those books on animals tomorrow," Eric said rather sheepishly, turned, and left the way he had come—through the ravine.

※　※　※

The next day he checked out four more books at the library, then hurried to keep an appointment he deeply hated: every other Thursday he had to go to the police station and tell a Sergeant Nolan what had he been doing. That was a condition of his probation. He really hated going in there and seeing all the cops grinning as he approached the sergeant's desk. They thought it was funny, but he sure didn't. And it was no picnic sitting there looking at Nolan's fat red face, and ticking off how many times he had been to the movies or the pool or Larry's. It was always the same routine. It was today, too. Just as Eric expected, the officer at the front desk grinned when he asked for Sergeant Nolan. Called from the front bench, he walked the gauntlet of smiles and snickers and plunked himself down in front of the sergeant, who finished perusing a file before swiveling around.

"Well, Eric, here you are."

"Yes, sir."

Sergeant Nolan cupped the thick folds of the back of his neck in both hands and gently swiveled as Eric reported on his activities the last two weeks. He claimed as usual not to have had any contact with Bones—a lie, since they met every day at Larry's.

The sergeant yawned predictably and leaned forward. "Okay." He tapped his pencil against the pile of books that Eric had placed on the desk. "What are these?"

"Books about animals," Eric said with a touch of pride.

"Yeah? You interested in that?"

"Sort of." Then he realized that he had not mentioned Mister Beck or the garden. He hadn't kept it back intentionally; it hadn't occurred to him that an old man would be important to a cop. Eric felt a sudden desire to talk about Mister Beck, this man whom he had been seeing for almost two weeks. He had never spoken of him to anyone until this moment. He mentioned Mister Beck out of an impulse of sheer enthusiasm. "I met this old man," he said, "who's got me interested in a garden."

"Yeah?" The sergeant yawned again. "Old man?"

"He sits all day in his garden," Eric explained eagerly. "He's teaching me how to look at it."

"Yeah?" The sergeant opened his sleepy eyes a little. "Teaching you what?"

"How to look at this garden. I don't know exactly what it means," admitted Eric, "but it's more interesting than you'd think."

"Yeah? Good," the sergeant observed indifferently. He pulled out the probation sheet from his desk, checked off the date, and initialed it.

"See you in two weeks," he said.

But Eric hadn't finished explaining about the old man. He felt that Sergeant Nolan didn't understand how strange and exhilarating the garden was. "Mister Beck wants me to know the name of every single thing in the garden," Eric continued. "He says I—"

"Beck?" Nolan sat upright.

"Yes, Mister Beck. He says I should—"

"Beck?" The sergeant swiveled around and spoke to another officer. "Hey, Danny. What's the name of that guy they let out of the state pen a couple of months back?"

"Who?"

"Came here to live with his daughter. In her custody. That old guy. From the state pen."

"Oh, him. Beck. Beck's the name."

Sergeant Nolan swiveled back to face Eric with a deep frown. "How did you meet this individual?"

"Mister Beck? I was walking through his garden and he spoke to me; that's all."

"And you hang around him?"

Eric bit his lip, wishing that he had been more cautious. "Not exactly."

"Look here, Eric, I'm going to tell you something. I don't want you hanging around this individual. Understand?"

"Yes, sir."

"Because he's a jailbird."

Eric felt his face getting hot. "You don't mean Mister Beck."

"That's who I mean. You stay away from him. I don't want a kid on probation mixing with jailbirds."

"Mister Beck?"

"You heard me."

"What did Mister Beck do?"

"Never mind. You just remember what *you* did," said Nolan, his eyes narrowing.

Eric got to his feet and gathered up the books. He felt the sergeant's eyes regarding him coldly. "Yes, sir," Eric mumbled and hurried out of there.

Once clear of the police station, Eric halted. Prison. So that was where Mister Beck had spent the last forty years.

When Eric climbed out of the ravine into the garden, Mister Beck was waiting.

"So you got the books," the old man said with a smile.

Eric tossed them down on the grass and stared at them, as if wanting to kick them.

"Something wrong?" asked Mister Beck.

"No."

"What's wrong, Eric?"

"Nothing's wrong." Eric shoved one of the books with his toe.

"Listen to me," said the old man. "And look at me."

Eric met the intense blue eyes.

"When something's wrong, tell me. If we can't be honest

with each other, you better pick up your books and leave right now."

Eric looked steadily at the old man. "Okay. I've got something to tell you."

"Shoot."

"I'm on probation."

Mister Beck placed a finger against his lower lip thoughtfully. "So that's it."

"I mean—*police* probation."

"What did you do?"

Eric told him.

"I see."

Eric studied the old man, who folded his hands on his lap and seemed untouched by the confession. "I want you to know," Eric said. "You said we ought to be honest."

"Yes, I should know," Mister Beck agreed, unfolding his hands and looking at them carefully. "And there's something you should know about me."

Eric nodded.

Mister Beck cleared his throat as if preparing to say something difficult. Eric knew, of course, what it was and waited for the old man to say it.

"You see, Eric," Mister Beck began after a long pause, "I'm sort of on probation, too—from a prison. I'm on parole."

Eric nodded.

"Did you already know it?" Mister Beck asked with a frown.

"I heard it at the police station."

The old man squinted hard, then slowly smiled. "Well, there it is," he said, opening his palms. "I did time in the state pen. A lot of time. Did the police tell you why?"

"They wouldn't tell me."

"I won't tell you, either," Mister Beck declared. "I suppose someday I will, but I won't now. Okay with you?"

"Okay."

"It's good we both cleared the air of this garden. Now let's get down to business." Mister Beck lifted a trembling finger. "Lie flat in the grass."

"What?"

"Lie flat on your stomach in the grass."

After a short pause, Eric did.

"Look around," the old man commanded.

Eric did.

"What do you see?"

"Grass." And Eric added, "the ground."

"Keep looking."

A couple of minutes passed.

Then the old man said, "Tell me now what you see."

"The same thing. Only—"

"Go on."

"I don't know," Eric said with a little laugh of self-consciousness.

"Go on."

"Well, everything seems bigger."

"Maybe that's because you're close to the ground, the grass."

"Like a—jungle." And it was true. With his face against the earth, his eyes at grass level, the longer Eric looked, the deeper into an endless undergrowth his eyes seemed to travel. It was an optical trick. He lifted his head quickly and stared at the smooth green lawn. For a few moments there he had lost his perspective.

"What made you look up?" asked Mister Beck.

"I felt a little funny."

"Take a break."

Eric shifted around into a sitting position, with the sunlight slanting across his legs making two shadows alongside them. He waited calmly for Mister Beck's next order. The past year in school he had waited in secret rebellion for commands he meant to follow only marginally, only enough to avoid trouble. Now, however, he leaned back with his hands flat on the warm grass and waited with a kind of lazy goodwill. He was encouraged by what had just happened; Mister Beck had asked him to do a very ordinary thing—lie down and look at the grass and the earth—but oddly enough, that ordinary thing had been different.

Abruptly Mister Beck said, "Find an ant and follow it."

Eric glanced around at the old man, who was grimacing impatiently. "You heard me," said Mister Beck. "An ant. Find one and follow where it goes."

Without a word Eric began crawling on all fours over the lawn. After only a few feet he saw a large black ant trundling between blades of grass. "Found one!" he shouted.

"Stay with it!"

Eric focused hard on the insect. He followed the six rapidly moving legs across clumps of earth, losing them momentarily under some crabgrass.

"Stay with it!"

Eric remained on all fours and peered so intensely at the ant from about a foot away that he began to feel dizzy. The machinelike rapidity of the black legs was hypnotic. He had to glance away a few times to clear his head so he could concentrate. And the ant's feelers, they, too, were hard to watch as they tapped, tapped, tapped, in all directions, wildly it seemed, like a garden hose at full pressure snaking from side to side. But he kept looking. He became aware of himself looking. He was not so much looking at the ant as thinking of himself looking at the ant. What would Superkool think of him crawling around in the grass after a little ant? What would Horse say? And Zap? What if the gang ever saw him down on his hands and knees, keeping a black ant in sight wherever it happened to go?

Eric blinked.

The ant was no longer there.

He searched the grass, swept his fingers through it, but the ant had definitely disappeared. "Lost it," he muttered.

"At least you kept it in sight for all of three minutes," Mister Beck observed.

"That's not long," said Eric, rising.

"Longer than you think. But have you any idea why you lost it?"

Eric shook his head.

"It can't be you lost the ant because it was too fast." Mister Beck waited. "Well, then?"

Eric shrugged.

"You started to think of something else, didn't you?"

"Yes."

"Maybe thirty seconds passed or even less. But that was enough time for the ant to hide or change direction. You were thinking about yourself looking at the ant."

Amazed at this insight, Eric stared at the old man, who was now smiling.

"Don't be surprised, Eric. When a man is locked up for forty years, he becomes acquainted with concentration. It's what he learns to do—concentrate—or he goes nuts. I lived in a cell, five by seven, so I learned how to expand it." Mister Beck stretched his trembling hands out as if to encompass the garden. "I lost myself in time and space." He squinted thoughtfully at Eric. "You have any idea what I'm saying?"

"Not exactly."

"That's right, but probably more of an idea now than you had before watching the ant. Here's what I did, Eric. I looked at a wall closely enough to find a crack in it, some kind of imperfection I could follow visually. I made my eyes follow that crack until it met another crack or the edge of the wall. Then I'd follow the new crack or the edge of the wall until something else crossed it, a new line of some sort. Pretty soon the wall became really immense. It was like a huge field or like this garden here, full of lines and bumps. It had character. It was like a face, full of variety and mystery. And for me, of course, the benefit was in the loss of time. Looking at a wall that way got rid of some hours—that many hours less to spend locked up. I had put them behind me without having to suffer through them. Kept me sane, Eric. But it took a long, long time before I could use the method without thinking about myself doing it. Go find another ant."

Eric found another ant without difficulty and followed it, but with the same result: He thought about something else just long enough for the ant to vanish. Again and again he tried, always losing the ant because his mind let the ant get away while his eyes were looking inward. Once he tracked one clear across the lawn before losing it in a flower bed.

"You stayed with that one almost ten minutes," remarked Mister Beck. "Damn good."

And so the afternoon wore on. Eric did not remember how many ants he followed until finally he stayed with one through a flower bed across the lawn into a nest near the foot of the pin oak.

"It's home!" he cried, peering down at the hole into which the ant had disappeared. Then Eric studied the route he and the ant had taken across the lawn, the forty feet or so that they had traversed together through endless time. His mind had veered away from the ant to himself, but never long enough to let the insect escape. Across the lawn, through a flower bed, into the ant hill. He had stayed with it all the way home.

Eric sat with his legs straight out, supporting himself on his elbows. The grass felt warm, cozy, and for some reason made him think of a wool blanket in winter. He stared into the blue sky. He breathed deeply, savoring the flower-ladened air.

"Eric?"

He turned toward the old man, who looked very solemn.

"I believe," said Mister Beck, "you're ready."

"For what?"

"To start looking at the garden."

Eric felt disappointed. "I thought that's what I've been doing."

"No, so far has only been a warm-up for the real thing.

That measuring tape I gave you—bring it tomorrow. I'll supply a ball of string."

"What's a ball of string for?"

"It's to help you get started."

Eric got to his feet. He didn't need his watch to tell him it was late. A long shadow extended from the old man in the chair; it was like a large black cutout lying on the lawn.

"Tomorrow," Mister Beck said and waved feebly.

Eric waved back and left. It occurred to him that the old man must be very tired after such a long day of work. Because it had been work. Both had been concentrating. Mister Beck had been concentrating on him concentrating, and that was hard work, too. At the edge of the garden he turned and called out, "Tomorrow!"

Slashing through the undergrowth of the ravine, Eric glanced around at a world that looked suddenly different. It seemed bigger and more complicated. Maybe this was because he had crawled around on all fours tracing the frenetic progress of an ant until finally it vanished into a hole. He could reach out on either side of the narrow path through the ravine and touch something alive, something that he might follow if he had enough concentration.

He felt a sense of triumph for having followed the ant so long.

Eric heard himself whistling.

※　※　※

When he opened the front door, Eric heard his mother calling from the living room. "Who is it? Eric? Come in here, please."

Eric found his mother sitting on a living-room couch; she

wore a pink evening dress. In front of her was a drink. That would be one of a number of concoctions she made for herself: fruit juices or vegetable juices. Father was in a tuxedo, holding his usual Scotch and water; in his lap lay a small notebook and his Texas Instrument Pocket Calculator. Deeply engrossed in a problem that would have to do with stock quotations, he kept punching keys rapidly.

"Where have you been?" Mother asked sharply and kneaded a handkerchief like a piece of dough.

"Around," Eric said. "I saw the sergeant," he added to placate his mother who seemed very nervous.

"I know you saw him. I got a call from him this afternoon," Mother said tensely. "Do you have any idea what he told me?"

Father glanced up from the calculator

Eric looked from one face to the other. "I guess so," he said lamely.

"Consorting with a known criminal," Mother said. "That's precisely how he put it."

Eric said nothing.

"Do you understand your mother?" Father asked quietly.

"Of course he does," said Mother. "Who *is* this man Beck?"

"Just someone I met."

"Ralph," said Mother. "Speak to him."

"The sergeant apparently told you, Eric, this man was in the state penitentiary."

"And only got out a few months ago," Mother added. She laughed bitterly. "No wonder he wouldn't join the Senior Citizens Club."

Eric said nothing.

"Well, say something! The man's a criminal," Mother affirmed in a rising voice of alarm.

"He's an old man." Eric plummeted down in a chair.

"I don't care," said Mother, twisting the handkerchief, "if he's a hundred years old. He's a criminal and, young man, you're on probation."

"He's eighty-two," Eric declared, meeting her eyes.

"That's hardly the point. The sergeant doesn't want you hanging around such a man, and neither does your father." She craned her head around Eric's chair to have a view of the doorway. "Roddy, go to your room. This doesn't concern you."

Eric did not need to glance back to have an image of his brother hastening away. Roddy had a gift for being on the spot when there was trouble.

"What I'm curious about," said Father, setting the calculator aside, "is your interest in this old man."

"Well, he knows a lot of things," replied Eric.

Mother guffawed. "I'm sure he does. How to rob banks. How to commit thefts."

"Is that what he did?" Eric asked.

"Don't tell me *you* don't know."

"Mister Beck didn't tell me."

"I can understand why."

"Did the sergeant tell you, Mother?" Eric persisted.

"No, he did not, so I suspect it was something terrible." Mother sighed and took a sip of her mixture of juices, which had assumed a purplish color.

"What I can't understand," she continued, "is how you could *find* such a person. Out of ten thousand people in this town, how could you manage to locate the particular one who just got released from prison?"

It was not a question Eric could answer. He sat there, hands on knees, waiting to be released.

"I don't think you quite understand," Father said. "It's the circumstance—you being on police probation—that makes this a serious matter. You vandalize your own school, then take up with a jailbird. How do you think that looks to people?"

"Do people know about Mister Beck?"

"The police do, and that's sufficient." Father picked up the calculator and stared thoughtfully at Eric. "We're counting on you to see the situation clearly. It's so obvious. Just stay away from Mister Beck, and we won't talk about it again. Okay?" He glanced down at his calculator.

Eric rose and observed Mother beginning to smile in relief.

"I'm glad that's over," she said and picked at the lacy edge of her evening dress. Since Mother had become a committee woman, there were dinner parties every week. "I'm glad you will listen to reason, Eric," she said. "Because this past year—I don't know—you haven't been yourself."

Eric said, for want of something better, "Don't worry about me. I'm all right."

Then Mother in a relaxed voice gave him instructions about the evening: There was a casserole in the warming oven; Susan would be sleeping at a friend's house, so she wouldn't be home for dinner; he was to see that Roddy got to bed by ten o'clock.

At ten thirty that night, when Roddy got to bed, Eric

decided to do some reading, instead of watching the late show. He took one of his library books, *Insect Life,* from his book shelf and went to his desk.

"Who is Mister Beck?" Roddy asked suddenly.

Eric glanced at the bed where Roddy sat bolt upright, his eyes shining. "None of your business."

"What are those books for?"

"What books?"

"The ones you brought home tonight."

"None of your business," replied Eric curtly. Lately books had been getting him into trouble: first Superkool, then Nolan, and now Roddy had all discovered something suspicious about his books.

"You never tell me a thing," grumbled Roddy. "Peter Brooks's brother—that's Keith, he's in the class ahead of you—he hits fly balls for him every afternoon. It's why Peter can catch so good."

Eric opened *Insect Life* and placed a dictionary on the desk beside it.

"So does Van's brother." Roddy waited, then asked in a high petulent voice, "What's the name of that book?"

Eric glanced sideways at his brother and wished he could confide in Roddy. A year ago they had been pals of a sort, but lately it seemed as if he had become older and Roddy had become younger. They had so little in common these days. All that Roddy seemed interested in was baseball statistics and hitting fly balls in the yard.

"Okay," grumbled Roddy, turning toward the wall. "Don't tell me. I know anyway."

Eric said, "It's a book about insects."

"I know. Only you could of told me."

"I didn't think you were interested in insects."

"I didn't think you were, either," Roddy retorted with his face to the wall.

There was nothing more to say; age had put a barrier between them. Eric read the first sentence in the book: "The animals of the phylum Arthropoda are commonly called arthropods. The name is derived from the Greek term *arthron,* joint, and *pous,* foot, having reference to the jointed feet."

Eric sighed. This was going to be tough going, but he resolved to plow through each and every one of the five hundred pages.

Inside the Squares 🌿

In the morning he had to control an impulse to race out of the house with the measuring tape in his pocket and make for the garden where Mister Beck must already be waiting, holding the mysterious ball of string. But Eric knew if he showed too much eagerness to leave the house, he would draw unwanted attention to himself. He didn't want to rock the boat. And at breakfast, much to his relief, there was no mention made of the criminal Mister Beck. Eric was all smiles and very polite to Susan, who had come home from her friend's house for breakfast. He figured he had better placate her, since traditionally she was his most implacable foe in the family. Not that she said or did much. It was the way she looked at him with a kind of amused contempt that unsettled him. He had seen her smile at other boys his age in the same way, keeping her best smiles naturally for boys her own age or older. Eric figured her for one of those people who have contempt for what they have just passed through themselves. But whatever the reason, she was al-

ways looking for signs of weakness in him and then pounc-
ing. He gave her a brilliant smile of welcome this morning.

In the course of breakfast conversation Mother asked him
what his plans were for the day. Not sure how innocent the
question was, Eric decided to be cagey. He said he was
going to meet the guys at the pool. He knew that Mother
took pride in his swimming skill. Moreover, she approved
of him meeting the guys, since she only knew of them
through their parents, all solid citizens, and did not know
that the other boy on probation was one of them. She was
not aware that they, along with Eric, formed an antisocial
element in school. In the old days, before her committee
work took so much time, she might have found out, but
now, harassed, she took for granted that boys of good family would be good companions. Fooling Mother was not
what gave Eric the most pleasure. Being different from
what she thought he was—that provided the little jolt of
satisfaction he felt each time she judged him wrongly.

This morning, after their parents and Roddy had left the
the house, Eric and Susan faced each other across the breakfast table.

"I heard about your criminal," she said with a smile.

"Who told you? Roddy?"

Susan did not reply. She had a skillful way of drawing him
into a situation, then backing out of it herself. Pouring yet
another cup of coffee, Susan stirred more cream into it than
a dieter should. She looked a little fat to Eric, who could
never understand why the girl got so many dates. But then
Father seemed to think she was pretty. When Mother became critical of Susan's weight, Father would always say,
"Ah, let her alone. Suzy's just pleasingly plump."

Now Eric felt her eyeing him thoughtfully. Looking up from his toast and jam, he was not comforted by her smile. It was not the smile of amused contempt; this was different. This was the smile of sly analysis. Susan wanted something.

And he was right. Abruptly she said, "Do me a favor?" Her voice was breathy; Eric had heard her use it with dates.

"What is it?" he asked cautiously.

"If you see Danny Richmond, say hello for me."

Danny Richmond was a lifeguard at the public pool—tall, blond, and a college student.

"Sure, if I see him," Eric promised, having no intention of seeing Danny Richmond at the pool. It was a gray area of honor: he wouldn't go to the pool, but if he did, he would say hello for Susan to Danny Richmond. The thing was, Eric believed in keeping a promise. A couple of years ago Mother had forced Father into promising to take him somewhere, and Father hadn't done it. Eric had long forgotten where Father had promised to take him, but his sense of disappointment and betrayal at Father's having failed to keep that promise was still fresh, still a wound he carried with him. So he would keep his promise to Susan —if by a miracle he was put into the situation to keep it.

"Promise," Susan insisted.

"Promise."

"I'll do you a favor back someday."

"I'll do it without payment," Eric responded sharply. "I mean, if I see him."

Susan's eyes narrowed. "You'll see him all right, if you really are going to the pool."

"Okay, then I'll tell him."

"Are you going to the pool?"

"You heard me say so."

Susan had a tinkling laugh, but it contained no mirth. Her laugh sounded to Eric like a snort of derision.

"What's funny?" he asked.

"Well, you can hardly expect me to believe you just because you told Mother. This is Susan, little brother."

Eric kept his expression impassive, although he winced inside and Susan knew it every time she called him "little brother." He got up and headed for the door at a deliberately slow pace, hands in pockets. Susan would detect the slightest eagerness.

"Sorry," he heard from behind him. Turning, he saw his sister give him a brilliant smile.

"I really am sorry," she told him. "Promise you'll say hello for me? Don't say any more, though. Don't look eager about it. Just say my sister Susan said to say hello. Leave it at that, okay?"

"Okay." Eric smiled and trailed over his shoulder the half-whispered words, "If I see him."

꙼ ꙼ ꙼

On the table lay a ball of twine next to the daily pitcher of lemonade.

"What was that area of the garden again?" Mr. Beck asked, squinting through the sunlight.

Eric checked the notebook which he always carried with him these days: 2,856 square feet.

Mister Beck asked him to find out how many six-foot squares would go into that area.

Eric sat cross-legged in the grass and set to work. Aside from simple arithmetic, it wasn't often that he had any reason to work a problem in math. Once he found the area of a six-foot square, he could divide the total area of the garden by that sum. As he was doing it, he saw from the corner of his eye Miss Beck backing out of the garage in a small car. Seeing him, she paused at the wheel. He could feel her eyes meet his; it was almost like a sound, like the crackle of electricity. It was a physical thing, their dislike for each other. She gunned the car and backed out rapidly. Then Eric finished his work. Holding up the notebook and waving it back and forth, he said confidently, "Seventy-nine squares!"

With a curt nod Mister Beck accepted the figure. "Seventy-nine," he repeated. "Let me see—" He closed his eyes and pursed his lips. "If you spend one hour in each square, and if you do, say, two or three squares each day, it will take about a month, maybe six weeks, to cover the entire garden." He shifted his gaze from empty space to the boy; his blue eyes had a burning intensity, as they studied Eric. "Because that's what you're going to do—spend an hour in each one."

Eric didn't understand; the squares were in his notebook, not in the garden.

"Got to start you in an interesting square," observed Mister Beck. "Can't let you get discouraged in a tough one either—say, one in the middle of the lawn." The old man put both hands on the arms of his chair and slowly pushed himself up.

Eric took a step forward, but the old man shook his head fiercely.

Like a branch in the wind Mister Beck trembled and shook throughout his body in an effort to rise from the

chair. Half erect, one hand gripping the chair arm, he gestured impatiently at the cane lying at his feet. Eric bent
instantly and snatched it up. The old man took it from him
with a determined frown, drilled its end into the earth, and
carefully started to lean upon its walnut head. The cane
wobbled but held up his weight, so with a little grunt of
decision he let go of the chair. For a few moments he
appeared to be suspended between balance and collapse,
his eyes fixed at a spot in the distance in pure concentration.

Eric had known that Mister Beck was old, of course, but
not *this* old. It was awesome, kind of frightening, and truly
bewildering, because to him the old man seemed at once
vulnerable and strong. Just rising from the chair took immense effort, yet the fact that Mister Beck could succeed in
that effort was proof of his having summoned a tremendous
power from within the frail body.

Eric watched without moving as the old man stepped
away from the chair, one big heavy shoe lifting and going
beyond the other in slow but spasmodic action.

Mister Beck halted after a dozen such difficult steps and
leaned with both weathered hands on the cane, facing the
clapboard house. He was taller upright than he had appeared to be in the chair, but terribly bent and even skinnier
now that he stood on those long shaky legs. His Adam's
apple stuck out prominently on the thin neck. His grizzled
chin thrust forward, his eyes squinting, Mister Beck continued to search for something in the morning light. At last,
with a trembling finger, he pointed to the southwest corner
of the house.

"There," he gasped. "Now help me back."

Eric rushed forward and held out his hand, which Mister

Beck refused. Instead, the old man laid his own hand on the boy's shoulder and maneuvered himself forward on the cane, talking in a breathless whisper: "Whittle four pegs to hold the lines of string. Cut the string and tie it to the pegs. Cut the string so it's six feet long between pegs." Mister Beck halted to catch his breath.

"It's hell being old," he said, finally sinking with a loud expulsion of air into the seat again.

In half an hour, following instructions, Eric had completed the task of cutting the string into four lengths and tying them to pegs of poplar branches. Next to the old man's chair he stretched out the string, sunk the pegs into the ground, and measured the distance between them with his steel tape. The string and pegs outlined a square, six feet by six feet.

"Good," said Mister Beck with pursed lips. "Now take the whole thing over to the southwest corner and peg it down."

Eric did. He studied the space enclosed by the white lines stretched tight between the pegs.

"Now climb inside," Mister Beck commanded.

Eric turned quizzically. "Climb inside?"

"That's what I said. Climb inside that square and sit down."

Eric did.

Sitting with his back toward the square, Mister Beck had to crane his neck around to see Eric. "Stay inside there one hour. Then pull the pegs up along one side and move them over to make an adjoining square. Got that?"

Eric nodded.

"Then climb inside that new square and stay one hour."

Mister Beck was facing straight ahead, so he no longer saw Eric. It seemed to Eric that the old man had turned away as an act of faith; it was like saying he trusted Eric to follow orders without being watched. "One square after another," Mister Beck continued, "until you cover the whole garden. Seventy-nine squares of it."

Eric said nothing. He was sitting cross-legged in the square, looking at a privet bush on his right side, with the full garden ahead, the Beck driveway on the left, and the rear of the house at his back.

"Tell me when you're ready to begin," said Mister Beck. "At first at least we better time each square exactly. I'll keep time."

"But—" Eric looked around wildly. He felt as though someone had just slammed the door, shutting him in a dark closet. "What am I supposed to *do* in here?"

"What do you think?"

"I don't know."

"You're in there for one hour. What are you going to do about it?" Mister Beck asked sharply.

"I don't know!"

"I thought we agreed about you looking at the garden."

"Well, yes—"

"So do it. Look at it. Look inside the six feet of it belonging to you right now."

"What belongs to me?"

"The six-foot square you're inhabiting. For the next hour it's the whole damn world!"

Eric glanced at each of the four strings.

"This is only a suggestion," continued Mister Beck, "but it would be a waste of your hour to spend most of it looking outside the square. Take advantage of the square you're in. And get a view of the world above it."

Without seeing the old man's face, Eric had the peculiar feeling that the words were coming from the air, from the sunlight, that they weren't spoken by a person. He regarded the white string suspiciously. What did the old man mean by this square being the whole world? The world as Eric had always thought of it was something big, generally in the shape of a globe like the planet Earth. But this six-foot square?

Eric squinted at the cloudless blue sky. "Get a view of the world above it," Mister Beck had said. Did he actually mean the air above this six feet of ground? Was the idea to concentrate on the exact overhead area of sky which corresponded to the little patch of earth on which he sat?

Eric glanced at his crossed legs, his jeans, his tennis shoes, at his hands playing idly across the top of the grass. Was he crazy to do this?

"Ready?" Mister Beck boomed out.

Eric started, as if shaken from a deep sleep. Then he felt his heart beating fast, a dryness in his mouth, as if he were beginning a cross-country race. "Ready!" he cried.

"Then start."

Eric found himself smiling, then laughing inwardly. Because this was really strange. Start what? No crowd was shouting. He wasn't running down a track or swimming the length of a pool. He was sitting where he had been before Mister Beck called out, "Then start." Eric's first reaction was to wait for something definite to happen—for Mister Beck to tell him what to do or explain things to him. But as the silence lengthened, Eric realized to his disappointment that the old man was going to remain absolutely silent during the hour.

Mister Beck had isolated him within the square.

Eric became acutely conscious of sitting motionless in the grass, so he moved his feet apart and then together, as if doing calisthenics. Then he stood up, his mind experiencing a little tug of surprise as his body felt abruptly free. He surveyed the whole plot of ground within the white lines. His kingdom? Nuts. He flopped down violently on his stomach, the way he used to do as a small boy when he wanted to pout. He placed his cheek flat against the earth, as he had done yesterday to look at the ant. He eyed the grass from the distance of an inch. Soon a tiny insect alit on a blade of grass; it came out of nowhere, a green nub of a thing. Had he failed to see it alight, Eric would not have taken it for anything alive. He stared at the little bump on the blade of grass until he couldn't tell if it was part of the grass or really a living thing clinging there. But when he blinked, during the instant his eyes were closed, the bump disappeared. The insect was gone. That incredibly fast. Gone into the bright air.

Eric sat up and squinted beyond the enclosure of string at midges and flies dancing like dust particles above the lawn. There was a buzz near his left ear, so he flicked wildly at the side of his head. Something flashed like tinfoil, dipped toward the earth, and vanished. More buzzing. There were restless things everywhere. Plenty was going on. He scuttled over to the privet hedge against the south line of white string. Branches extended across the boundaries of his world. He put his nose against a twig to feel the tiny scratch of its bark. A bee hovered above the privet, its wings whirring so rapidly that they looked like a thin but solid veil—and vanished. There, then gone—and Eric hadn't the slightest idea where. He curled himself into a ball beneath the overhanging branches of the privet hedge. He let his sight travel slowly from the endmost leaf along a bough to another branch and then down the stem until the little trunk of the privet disappeared into black loam.

So he had looked at the square. So what? Eric sat back and expelled his breath in loud exasperation. He was disappointed. What had just happened? He had forced himself into visually tracing the shape of some branches on a hedge until they vanished into the ground. That's all. Nothing more. It was kind of stupid.

He glanced idly at the chair in the lawn. Just visible alongside the chair, from his vantage point, was a shapeless trouser leg, a shoe, a limp hand. Was the old man dozing? Probably. Probably Mister Beck was sound asleep like a child while Eric himself sat stupidly inside four pieces of white string pegged into the ground and did nothing. He felt betrayed. Mister Beck had led him to believe something important would happen if he sat in the square, but nothing had happened. Was it a joke? Was the old man having fun at his expense? Eric lay out full length and squinted at the sky partially obscured by the privet bush.

The blue patch overhead was cloudless, without interest. It was nothing to look at. Was he going to stay here for an hour? It was a loony thing to do. It was dumb. It was like —being in prison. Was that Mister Beck's idea, to give him a taste of prison?

A faint stir of wind agitated the branches, forming sudden intricate designs of leaf and twig against the flat blue background. Something moved on a branch. It was an ant, moving along the stem and over the joint of each leaf. Like a physical blow, the thought came to Eric that the world of an ant was small. Of course, he had always known this, but somehow it was new to him now. Where leaf fitted into branch, there was a large bump—at least to the ant—like a huge mound of thick solder looming ahead that must be traversed, as the ant journeyed endlessly along the road leading to the far distant bottom of the valley where the immense trunk of the privet bush sunk its huge roots into the earth. The ant's feelers kept tapping. The insect must not see very well or far, and it had that great journey to take before reaching solid ground. For a couple of seconds Eric felt as though he lived in the black skull of that tiny creature, peering from its globular eyes at the gigantic world.

Then the magic moments passed. Eric sat up again and glanced aimlessly at privet bush, grass, strings, at the figure obscured by the back of the chair. The sun, wheeling, began to throw a shadow into the thirty-six feet of his world. He watched the shadow slide like dark oil into his territory, across his right side, his left side, and ooze onward beyond the boundary of string. The soundless progress of the shadow was calming and pleasant. The square now felt much bigger than it had when first he stepped inside. A nearby rustle startled him. There it was, a tiny brown bird gripping a branch of privet. It had a saucy blue eye that turned rapidly in its socket, round and alert in every direction. The small creature balanced, tilted, and with a motion beyond Eric's capacity to follow, was again airborne, its wings in a furious whirr. Eric flopped upon his stomach, keeping his head high enough for him to have a skimming view of the top of the grass. In a matter of seconds he observed at least a half-dozen leafhoppers leaping through his kingdom. How long had he been in the square? Eric had sworn to himself not to look at his watch, but curiosity was too much for him—he raised his wrist and in shocked dismay realized that only twenty minutes had gone by. He had expected—had hoped—for much longer. He just might not hold out for a full hour if he didn't find something to do, so he decided to play a game to pass the time.

He would take a census of his country. Crawling to one corner of the square, he began to count anything that was alive. Some time later—he did not glance at his watch—he lost count at about fifty insects; there were just too many of them passing in view for him to keep track. And he had crawled through only about a third of the square. He decided to add a new element to the game: he pretended to be a reconnaissance plane spotting for ground troops in enemy territory. It was kind of childish, something that Roddy might do, but there was not much choice there in the string-enclosed patch of grass. So beginning again at the corner, he pretended to stare through binoculars from the plane at the dense jungle below. He saw plenty of troops and equipment—insects of all kinds—moving through the undergrowth. Then he gave up the game altogether, because his interest shifted from the childish fantasy to the very real life going on down there at ground level. He knelt and looked until his back ached from the strain of holding such a tense position. He had never examined anything in his life as closely as he did the little patch of earth within four pieces of string.

What seemed at first to be rumpled bits of soil upon

closer examination turned out to be a nit or bug or minuscule ant or something else—something alive and with legs —or a filmy spider no larger than a pinhead and as light and delicate as dust. The surface of a small wrinkled globe of black fruit, which had fallen from the privet bush, seemed to be liquidly in motion, until he realized with astonishment that tiny things were actually crawling upon it, the myriads of them being the real cause of the motion. Once he scratched a mound of earth about the size of his thumbnail only to discover that it was in truth the dried corpse of a fly mingled with dirt, and looking closer, he noticed something churning inside the fly, something alive but much too small for him to know more about it than that it was alive.

He decided then to finish the game, although he had long since given up any hope of counting the enemy troops. With his chin nearly touching the grass, he inched his way along, pretending to observe the hostile territory from the reconnaissance plane, searching each swell and dip of ground, each broken twig or nubbin of stone, for a sign of squirming life. And then his mind wandered away from the game again, again returned. His attention was like a tennis ball volleyed across a court. Suddenly he lifted his head and gazed across the white string at the real garden.

The real garden.

Because everything beyond the string now seemed real, whereas everything within it was outsized, tangled, creeping, prolific, wild, and restless, confusing his mind with things that vanished, that were not there or that changed, that were enemy troops one minute and midges the next. The world of the square was indeed a place of unexpected encounters and strange motion. The tiny life streaming through the green undergrowth did not yield its presence without a visual struggle on his part, and when he became aware of it, it disappeared—or even bored him, once he felt the victory of discovering it. A couple of times he was seized by panic. He sat bolt upright. An hour? He was going to sit first here and then in seventy-eight other squares for that long? He looked at the strings surrounding him and imagined they were magnetic fields—lethal. If he put one toe or finger beyond one of them, he'd be electrocuted. He didn't know if he was bored or scared. He didn't feel exactly like himself. He felt spread out at one moment and disconnected the next, because he had become excruciatingly conscious of time passing and himself sitting in this small space. Was it like prison? Had Mister Beck felt as strangely? But if Mister Beck had felt it, there had been no way for him to escape, whereas Eric could always rise and step over the string and be free. He toyed with the idea of doing just that—stepping easily across the string and striding without a word out of the garden. He recalled something then from the distant past, from his early childhood. He had been watching the flame waver blue and yellow on the stove burner. He had been old enough to know that he could get burned if he thrust his hand into that circle of flame, yet he almost did it. He had felt his hand trembling with anticipation; then the moment had passed, and both hands plunged into his pants' pockets.

He actually got up and stood at the border of the square, looking down at the taut string. One step and he'd be free. Free of what? He couldn't be hurt by remaining inside, so he had no reason to fear the passing minutes. He had no reason to fear Mister Beck and the method of looking at things, either. It wasn't freedom he would find by stepping over the line—it would be the burning flame, the pain of failure.

Turning around, he put his back at the string and flopped down again into the grass. How warm and ticklish it felt against his skull. The grass went on endlessly, beyond the limits of his body that rested upon it. He could see it in his mind's eye rolling into the distance like a great green rhythmic breaker, the kind he had seen that time when the family went to the beaches of Florida a couple of years ago.

Then he heard the powerful voice which always sounded so peculiar, coming as it did from such a frail old man: "Time's up!"

Eric leaped to his feet and vaulted the string in one bound and rushed to the chair, grinning in triumph.

Mister Beck gave him a thoughtful frown. "Well, what do you say?"

"I did it."

"Of course you did. You stayed the full hour. But tell me what happened."

Eric told him about counting the insects but failing because there were so many of them. He recited then a fact he had memorized from the insect book: one species of fly, if all its young lived to full growth for a single year— figuring one eighth of a cubic inch per fly—would cover the earth with its offspring at the end of that year to a depth of forty-seven feet. Mister Beck smiled at this information in a way that told Eric that the old man understood how difficult had been the process of memorizing it.

"Did you get bored?" Mister Beck asked suddenly.

"Sort of."

"You can't sit in a plot of ground that small for that long and not feel a little boredom. Panic?"

Eric nodded.

The old man nodded back as if satisfied. "Go get the ice tray from the refrigerator. The lemonade got warm."

When Eric was returning from the house with the ice tray, he noticed Mister Beck slipping a couple of pills into the pale-lipped mouth.

Old blue eyes met his. "Get my age and you become a pill taker, Eric. These make me drowsy, so if I conk out while you're sitting in a square, you time yourself."

Eric wanted to know what the pills were for, but it was the sort of question that Mister Beck might resent. There were limits he mustn't cross with someone as private as the old man. And yet Eric had glimpsed something disturbing —a grimace flicker across the wrinkled face of Mister Beck. It could mean pain. It probably did mean pain. Eric figured the little white pills helped to deaden it.

While pouring the lemonade, Eric thought about getting old. He hoped that he wouldn't live long enough to get as old as Mister Beck. His father's age was about as far as he wanted to go. Father could still play a game of tennis on weekends, although that probably wouldn't last much longer, and then Father would look more and more like Grandfather, and finally like Mister Beck. No, Eric didn't want to live that long and take pills and feel pain.

※　※　※

In the days that followed, Eric moved from south to north, from west to east, sitting in each square until he had covered nearly a third of the garden. Each evening after dinner he went to his room and read the books. He learned to distinguish between a centipide and insect, between a bug and a beetle, and he stored away some exotic facts, such as that the queen termite can lay sixty eggs per second. In the intervals between sittings, he carried the books around the garden and through illustrations identified stone flies, aphids, wood thrushes, and grackles. He observed earthworms wriggling through the grass and nasty-tempered starlings splashing in the birdbath. He learned to take the world into himself as it wished to come, while eluding boredom and fending off panic. For example, he'd watch a trail of tiny red ants moving in and out of a crack in the side board of the house, where wood grain rippled soundlessly, and he'd just go along with the stream of them, not trying to prove anything by watching them, not even wondering where so many of them were heading with such determination, but he would just look, just let his eyes and the ants do the work.

And yet a feeling of disappointment began to intrude upon Eric's experience of the garden.

He felt at times that he was faking his interest in it.

His real pleasure was in talking with Mister Beck because the longer he knew the old man, the more he liked him. Eric yearned to ask personal questions in spite of his respect for the old man's privacy. Now and then, between sittings, he managed to overcome his timidity and get a reminiscence out of Mister Beck. He'd loll in the grass next to the big black shoes from which the thin legs protruded, the skin above the socks all mottled and flecked with white hairs, and he'd squint up at the grizzled face from which a powerful voice boomed out descriptions of faraway places: Bangkok, Kamakura, Singapore, where Mister Beck had gone as a sailor before Eric's own father had even been born. Infrequently the old man gave a fleeting but terrible description of prison life. He stared into the garden air as if seeing it all again: the barred window of his cell, the cot, the sink, the toilet without a seat, the unshaded light bulb dangling overhead.

And then he mentioned his paintings.

During his later years in prison he had been allowed to keep a sketch pad, then oils and small canvases in his cell.

"Started as a hobby," Mister Beck explained. "Then it got serious with me. I worked all the time at it. Got some of the work inside the house," Mister Beck said proudly. "Show you one of these days."

Eric wanted to see the paintings immediately, but did not ask. It was strange how he and Mister Beck were with each other. They were not formal, but they kept clear of most things that didn't involve the garden. Mister Beck, for example, had never asked him a single question about his family. Life for the two of them seemed to begin only when he climbed the ravine into the garden.

"Don't mind admitting," continued Mister Beck, "some art dealers came to the prison just to see my work." He guffawed. "As a matter of fact, I'm expecting one to come here and take another look."

Eric regarded the white tufts of hair on either side of the suntanned skull. What was inside that head? What had those fiercely blue eyes seen? Often Eric was tempted to ask about the prisoners. What had the dangerous convicts—the murderers—been like? And the guards? Had there been riots in the prison? And attempted escapes? Had Mister Beck tried and been caught? Had he?

Eric began to regard Mister Beck as a lonely adventurer, a glamorous outcast, perhaps a colorful thief, a bold spirit contemptuous of ordinary life. So engrossed did Eric become in his imagined portrait of the old man that the hours within the squares had less appeal than the intervals outside them, when he could drink a glass of lemonade and hope for another revelation from Mister Beck's past.

It got to the point that Eric could hardly face the prospect of sitting in a square. But worse than his impatience with the garden was his faked enthusiasm for it. He must not cheat this old man. It was wrong; it was worse than breaking windows.

꽃 꽃 꽃

A couple of weeks after he had started on the squares, Eric awoke one morning from a strange dream. In it he ran amok in The Lonely Hunter while Miss Beck stood helplessly behind the counter and watched him smash vases, overturn tables, rip apart bedspreads, grind trinkets underfoot, hurl ashtrays through the plate-glass windows. And then he was being shoved into a patrol car, grinning, while photographers snapped his picture.

He rolled over in bed and blinked into the morning light. Cocking an ear, he listened for sounds downstairs. Silence. The clock on his desk indicated ten o'clock. Everyone had left the house long ago. Eric had sat up long past midnight, reading the book on insects. He had fallen asleep sitting up, somewhere around page 450. The book now lay beside him. Eric picked it up and on sudden impulse threw it across the room. He didn't want to be reminded of the garden this morning. Insects were okay, but not those he saw within the squares, because he hated the squares. The possibility occurred to him that he might announce to Mister Beck his decision never to sit in a square again. He imagined the scene. He said, "I like you, Mister Beck, and I like coming here to listen to you talk. About going to sea and being in prison. That's what really interests me, not this garden. So let's give up this business of me sitting in the squares." And Mister Beck nodded solemnly and replied, "That's all right with me, Eric."

Only Mister Beck would not really say that. He'd probably ignore the little speech and ask Eric to begin: "Are you at square twenty-three today?"

With a sigh Eric got out of bed, dressed, and went downstairs. Making himself toast and warming up the coffee, he watched the TV soap opera for the first time in many days. Not much had changed; the crises and relationships had remained intact: this person was crazy, that one in love, this one out of love, this one going to court, that one to the hospital. He yawned, feeling tired and lazy, perhaps because Father had ordered him to mow the lawn today. Although a professional gardener came in twice a week to tend Mother's flowers, the task of mowing the lawn—at Father's insistence—was reserved for Eric. "The least he can do," Father often observed, and Mother agreed, because aside from this business of mowing the lawn, Father left the control of Eric's life to Mother.

Tired, lazy. But Eric went outside to the toolshed behind the garage. It was filled with machine tools purchased by Father last year in a burst of enthusiasm for taking up woodworking as a hobby. That notion had lasted a week, as all such notions did; Father discovered as usual that there wasn't time after his daily schedule of work to do anything more than eat dinner and slump down half-asleep in front of the television. So now the tools hung on nails and the new workbench stood unmarked. Eric ran his fingers idly along its smooth wood surface. Instead of looking at a garden, he might take up woodworking himself and make Roddy a baseball bat, Susan a dresser. Fat chance of that.

Eric pushed the power mower from the shed and wheeled it into the backyard. He noticed the next-door neighbor sitting under a striped umbrella. Mrs. Wilson wore a cotton dress; her bare feet with crimson toenails were propped on a stool. He could see the freckles on her arms all the way across the yard. There was a tall glass beaded with moisture on the table beside the chair.

Mrs. Wilson was already at the booze, although the sun had not yet risen above the eastern trees.

"Ric!" she called and waved gaily. "Hey, kid, come over and have a little drink!" It was what she always said. And she wasn't joking, either; Eric knew if he ever took up the offer, Mrs. Wilson would give him as much, as often, as he wanted.

Mrs. Wilson was about Mother's age, childless, a rich woman whose husband was rarely home. Eric felt sorry for Mrs. Wilson, the freckled woman with painted toenails and nothing to do all day but sit under the lawn umbrella and consume whiskey. He walked into her yard and halted a half-dozen feet away from her. "Hello, Mrs. Wilson," he said, aware that he had nothing to add. He had just gone over there on impulse, because she looked so lonely with her feet propped up on the stool, with bright red nail polish on her toes, and nowhere to go.

"How about that drink?" Mrs. Wilson asked, grinning.

Eric smiled.

"Hell, I mean it," slurred Mrs. Wilson. Her mouth was smeared unevenly with lipstick. "Bottle's next to the sink. Go on."

"No, thanks."

Mrs. Wilson shrugged and regarded him curiously. "Hear you're on probation."

Eric nodded.

"What did you do that was so awful?" she asked, smiling.

Eric told her.

"Why in hell did you do that, Ric?"

Whenever he had been asked that question, Eric had always given a pat reply: "I don't know." And in fact he hadn't known exactly. But there was a kind of easy freedom about Mrs. Wilson that allowed him to relax enough to consider a better answer. So he said, "I'm going into high school next year."

She waited, cocking her head.

"This other kid and me got to thinking about it." He paused.

"Didn't make sense, all that going to school. Is that right?"

"I guess so," he said, relieved to see that Mrs. Wilson understood. "Then we got to thinking about junior high—it all seemed stupid."

"And so you went over there and gave them hell." Mrs. Wilson guffawed and sipped from the glass. "Good for you," she said. "Better smash a few windows in life than sit

back and take it in silence. Or you'll end up with this stuff"
—she wiggled the glass in her hand—"if you sit back and
take it."

Eric waved and returned to his own yard. Glancing over
his shoulder, he saw Mrs. Wilson balancing the drink with
one hand on her ample stomach. Her painted toes glittered
in the slanting light.

Eric mowed the lawn. While guiding the mower across
the sweet-smelling grass, he kept thinking of the Beck garden. Why did he always imagine it as being larger than this
one, even when he knew his family's garden was almost
twice as big? Maybe he really did like the Beck garden.
Maybe, but he wasn't sure. At least he didn't want to sit in
any square today. He didn't want to cheat Mister Beck with
phony good cheer. If he ever sat in a square again, it would
be when he felt like it, when he wanted to do it. And so
instead of going to the Beck garden, he decided to go to
the public swimming pool where the gang hung out on hot
days. He put the mower away and glanced over at Mrs.
Wilson dozing under her umbrella, an empty glass beside
her on the table; Eric rode away on his bike, content with
his decision to stay away from the Beck garden. He owed
himself a day off, like a businessman sneaking away for a
game of tennis.

He pedaled downtown to the large municipal park, at
one end of which was the softball park where, at this very
moment, Roddy would be hitting fly balls, and at the other
end of which lay the fenced-in swimming pool.

Soon Eric was standing in blue trunks on hot cement at
poolside. He felt self-conscious in the presence of so many
people, many of them kids about his own age, sunning or

swimming in the frothy green water. It was one of the largest pools in the entire state, requiring three lifeguards on duty.

Eric shaded his eyes and scanned the chairs, looking for one of the lifeguards—Danny Richmond, Susan's new boyfriend.

And there was Danny, standing on a lifeguard chair and giving the crowd an unobstructed view of his bronzed thighs and muscled biceps. Staring at the powerful young man, Eric crossed his arms across his own thin chest. He never did like Susan's boyfriends; she always chose them for their looks. Glancing enviously at the lifeguard, Eric hugged his arms in his armpits, obscuring the thinness of his own chest. He didn't like Danny Richmond. And yet he had given his sister a promise and must keep it. Of course, he had given the promise some time ago, and now that Susan and Danny were dating, it wasn't necessary to bring his sister to the college boy's attention. But a promise was a promise, so Eric walked over to the lifeguard chair, arms still hugging his chest.

"Hey," he yelled, squinting into the bright sunlight at muscles glistening from suntan oil. "Susan says to say hello!"

Danny Richmond peered down. "What?"

Eric repeated the message, then realized that Danny Richmond wasn't aware of his name. "I'm Eric Fischer, Susan's brother."

The strong young face of Danny Richmond broke into an enthusiastic smile. "Yeah, Eric—*swell.* Nice to meet *you.* And thanks. Thank her for *me,* will you?"

Thank her for having her brother say hello? The lifeguard's effusiveness convinced Eric that the guy had nothing but good looks; he was a dope, grinning like that over a simple hello.

Eric turned away contemptuously and put a lot of distance between himself and the Adonis on the lifeguard chair. In a far corner he flopped down and stretched out, making himself visually a small target for the alert gazes of girls he knew from school. Not having sunbathed in a couple of weeks, he was a little pale, except his face and hands, which were dark from sunning in the Beck garden. Glancing back in dismay at his legs, he saw they were much lighter than his hands, and so were his arms. He was striped like a zebra or something, and the thought of those girls judging him was almost enough for him to get up and leave.

Then across the thrashed pool he saw a familiar face. It was Silky, one of his schoolmates, cautiously testing the end of a diving board. The black boy jumped up and down a couple of times before springing high and performing an awkward swan dive.

Eric dove into the pool, too, and stroked toward the diving boards. He swam with pride, aware of the skillful coordination of his arms and legs. Swimming was the one athletic thing he could do without feeling ridiculous or incompetent. He reached the diving area in time to witness Silky take a belly flop from the high board. The cracking sound he made on entry had the whole pool looking in the direction of the diving boards. Silky's dark head appeared. He blew his breath out and grinned, then slowly breast-stroked over to the side of the pool.

Eric, who had got out, leaned down and gave Silky a hand.

"How'd you like that one?" Silky asked with a broad smile, as he took Eric's hand and climbed out of the pool.

"You'll get it right." Eric studied the catlike agility with which the black kid walked over to the fence and sat down. Silky was a good athlete and a whiz at chemistry. He had also been a disappointment to a lot of kids when six months ago he came to town from Chicago. There weren't many blacks in town, and people at school had expected him to be a tough urban kid who would tell them about gangs in the inner city. Silky came from the inner city all right, but he never talked about gangs. That was why Superkool and Horse and the others disliked him. They had expected him to hang around with them, whereas Silky had chosen to join the track team and the math club and the debating society.

Eric and he sat against the wire fence, analyzing the diving styles of other kids. Silky was a methodical observer, noticing if the diver made his release close to or far from the end of the board and started a maneuver too soon or too late. Eric knew that it wouldn't take Silky long to become a first-rate diver.

"What you doing this summer?" Silky asked.

"Nothing much."

"I'm playing a lot of tennis, so I got to pay for it."

"Do you like living here?"

"It's okay," said Silky. "I'm into it now. What about you? How you doing?"

Eric knew he meant the probation. "It's stupid going to the cops every two weeks and telling them I'm a good boy."

Silky laughed. "It won't last forever." He sat up straight and stiffened. "Here's where I get off," he said and rose.

Silky was looking across the pool at the entrance of the

Men's Dressing Room. There stood Horse, big and power-ful, with Zap, a head shorter and twenty pounds lighter, at his side.

The guys saw Eric and waved, then dove into the pool. Silky began walking away.

"Where you going?" Eric asked.

Silky halted and stood a moment with hands on his hips, grimacing. "Where *they* aren't. I don't know why you hang out with them, Eric, but I'll tell you one thing—I won't."

"They're not so bad."

"No, not so bad," countered Silky and turned away. Over his shoulder he added, "Just dumb."

They were not dumb, either, thought Eric. They were just not as serious as Silky was, but maybe they were more honest than Silky because unlike him they refused to play the game at school. Eric watched them swim across the pool —Horse in the lead, flailing the water with his big arms, and Zap wagging his head awkwardly from side to side.

Then they were climbing out of the pool, and Eric braced instinctively, waiting for the inevitable blow that Horse would give him.

And it came, a stinging cuff on the arm, when Horse reached his side. "Where have *you* been!" Horse bellowed, making a grotesque face.

"I know," said Zap, grinning, his stray eye looking past Eric. "He's been reading about the birds and bees, flowers and trees. This guy's a real bookworm."

Solo expected this to happen. When Superkool had caught him with the books, Solo had known he'd have to pay for it. But that was just the gang's way of dealing with something new.

Horse poked him hard in the chest with one finger. "What's with you anyway? Lost your marbles? Gonna join the bird watchers?"

Zap was giggling.

"Gonna plant a garden in your armpits?" With each fierce question Horse jabbed Solo in the chest, driving him toward the wire fence.

"Hey! You there!"—the rapid blowing of a whistle— "Stop that horsing around!"

It was Danny Richmond from the lifeguard chair across the pool. He held a whistle in one hand and a megaphone in the other. "Cut the horseplay!"

Zap snickered. "He knows your name, Horse."

The big fellow stepped clear of Solo and moodily drew his big fist across his mouth.

Solo slumped against the fence, grateful to Susan for having a lifeguard as a boyfriend. That Horse—sometimes he was too rough. He didn't mean anything; he was just so big that he hurt people without realizing it. But Zap was another story. Solo had seen him out of the corner of one eye, while Horse was poking brutally with that finger. Zap had enjoyed the pain Eric was feeling. The pleasure had shown on Zap's face. Of all the gang, Zap was the one Solo liked least. He feared Superkool and to a lesser extent Horse, but he felt that with a little effort he could dislike Zap a lot.

"Look!" cried Zap.

Standing at the shower-room entrance was another boy, muscular, with long blond hair—Superkool. He ran across the slippery cement—against the rules—and dove into the bright water.

"Let's go get him," muttered Zap.

The trio dove into the pool and set out for Superkool, whom they met midway. "Where have *you* been!" yelled Horse and splashed water in his face. The trio surrounded him and closed in.

"Hey, guys!" pleaded Superkool, with his long blond hair matted against his skull, giving him a girlish look. "Come on! Let me alone!"

Giggling, the trio lunged all at once. Superkool vanished under their onslaught. Sputtering and pleading for mercy, he tried to swim out of their reach, but Horse dragged him down again. He emerged gasping from the water and went under again.

The trio quit ducking him for fear of a blast from one of the lifeguards.

Solo felt good. He had pushed hard with his own hands against Superkool's broad shoulders and watched the blond head disappear into the swirling green water.

"Damn you guys," Superkool grumbled as they swam into the shallow area of the pool.

"Serves you right for showing up late," said Horse complacently.

Solo glanced around to see if anyone had watched them duck Superkool. A cluster of kids was staring. One of the kids was nearly Solo's height, but Solo felt much bigger because in the company of a guy as big as Horse he had helped to duck someone as strong as Superkool.

"What's that?" Superkool in waist-high water was pointing in the direction of a girl who was thrashing awkwardly around in an attempt to swim.

"That's some kind of a dog trying to swim," yelled Zap.

It was Sandra Gibson from school. A plump, timid girl who played trumpet in the band, she still wore long braids. A few times she had given Solo her class notes for English.

Superkool held his arms out wide, making claws of his fingers. Like a rampaging gorilla, he growled deeply in his throat. Seeing him lunge for her, the girl rapidly windmilled her feet to regain the bottom and stood up straight, arms crushed defensively against her chest. Superkool splashed water into her face, accurately, relentlessly. Up went her hands as she backpedaled toward the side of the pool. She never reached it. Horse, circling behind her, grabbed her by the neck and tumbled her into the water with one heavy hand, so that only her braids remained on the surface. The next moment Sandra shot up out of the water, gasping and scarcely getting a gulp of air before Zap plunged her down again. This time she came up sobbing, both hands gripping her face as if it were a mask she wanted to remove. Then, with the palm of his hand against the back of her neck, Superkool ducked her hard and held her for a few seconds before letting her bob up like a cork.

Then it was Solo's turn.

He glanced at Horse, whose lips parted in anticipation. Zap was giggling, bouncing up and down in the water. Solo lurched for the girl, trying to grab her arm, but it was too slick and his hand slid off. Then he reached for her face, half covered by her own hands, and was startled by the cold feel of her fingers against his own. This time he got a grip on her and pushed, almost frightened by the ease of toppling her. The girl had suddenly become withdrawn and passive, as if aware for the first time in her life that there were things you had to accept, had to suffer somewhere deep inside yourself. Solo pushed her down as far as he could. She did not resist, but went under as if on command, docilely. She came up sputtering when he released her. She came up soft, her hands still placid against her face, soundless, limp.

Solo was appalled by her acceptance of his violence. It was worse than if she had hit him. It made him ashamed and angry that she chose not to resist more. He could not duck her again, but stepped away and with the others splashed water on her plump arms, on the swim cap pulled awry, on the black tank suit.

"You!"—the sound of one whistle, then two blowing—"Hey!"

The four boys turned in the direction of the lifeguard chair nearest them. A tall guard was gesturing violently at them and blowing his whistle. From the other two chairs the other guards were doing the same—warning them to let the girl alone or get out.

The snickering boys scattered, leaving Sandra rubbing her eyes slowly and carefully as if trying to remove something sharp from them.

The boys regrouped at a corner of the metal fence, giving one another little punches of excitement. Solo even poked Horse, not hard, but he did it. He felt good; he felt bold and cruel and old. Sandra was standing against the scupper drain of the pool, eyeing the boys across the green water, while three of her girl friends gathered protectively around her and glowered at her attackers with moral indignation.

"Served her right," muttered Horse, looking at his knuckles as if they belonged to someone else and he was studying them for the first time with a kind of awe.

"Look at the dogs," said Zap, grinning back at the furious girls.

"Did you get it?" Horse asked Superkool, as they lounged nonchalantly against the fence.

"He didn't have any."

"What's this?" asked Solo. He could ask what he wanted to now; he had ducked that girl, and it made him one of them again in spite of his strange books.

"A guy said he could get us some grass. Only he couldn't," Superkool explained. "But—" he added, snapping his fingers, "we got a little something else. Come on, you guys."

The four boys skittered across the hot cement, slowing down for a few moments under the critical gaze of Danny Richmond, and then racing into the entrance of the Men's Dressing Room. Walking stiff-legged like robots, they entered the Basket Room, where Superkool asked the attendant for his clothes. "Got to get something," he explained apologetically when the attendant, an older boy, seemed puzzled by the request.

"Get something from what?" demanded the attendant, glancing at each dripping member of the quartet.

"My money," said Superkool. "I owe these guys on a bet. Please."

"Please," cooed Zap.

"Please," urged Solo and Horse in concert.

The older boy glared a moment, then took the numbered tag from Superkool's hand and matched it to a metal basket on the shelf. He pulled the basket out and with a little grunt of exasperation slid it onto the counter.

Superkool snatched it up and turned away.

"Find your money *here,*" said the attendant. "I'll put the basket back."

Superkool looked over his shoulder. Confused, he reddened. "What?"

"I'll put it back."

"Sure, only I got to take it inside and look. I don't know where I put the money."

The older boy opened his mouth to argue, but three kids carrying baskets emerged from the Dressing Room, so he forgot the suspicious quartet and took care of the new arrivals.

Superkool took advantage of this diversion to shoot into the Dressing Room, followed by the others, where he plunked down the clothes basket on a cement bench and performed a wild little dance of triumph. Humming a disco tune and wiggling his buttocks obscenely, he yanked an airline bag from under his crumpled pile of clothes. Opening the bag, Superkool paused and turned with a fanged smile and snarled fiercely at his companions.

"Come on," Horse muttered impatiently. "Quit the clowning."

Slowly, like a magician pulling a rabbit from a hat, Superkool pulled a bottle of whiskey from the bag.

"How much did the guy soak you for it?" asked Zap judiciously.

"Eleven bucks. You guys owe me."

"Eleven's too much," complained Zap. "He really soaked you. There's this guy who goes to State; he said he'd sell me a bottle for nine."

"Open it," demanded Horse, reaching for the bottle. Both he and Superkool grasped the neck of it for a few moments, then Horse's bigger hand came away with the bottle. Horse twisted the top off, glanced quickly at the Dressing Room entrance, then gloated at his companions, and lifted the bottle. His Adam's apple pumped a couple of times. He lowered the bottle, coughing and sputtering.

The boys giggled as Superkool reached for the bottle.

Horse pulled it in close to his chest. "I'm not through," he said in a strangled tone of voice. Lifting the bottle again, he gulped once, twice, three times until, coughing explosively, he sprayed whiskey across the bench. His eyes were watering. "Hey, that's good stuff," he whispered hoarsely and handed the bottle to Zap, who did not hesitate an instant, but lifted it and drink until he, too, sputtered.

The bottle went to Superkool. He contemplated the amber liquid in a humorous parody of a connoisseur, then did a little dance.

"Remember," he crowed, "you guys owe me!"

"Go on," grumbled Horse.

Superkool drank.

Then the bottle was shoved against Solo's chest. He took the bottle by the neck and glanced at two kids—about eight or nine—who stood watching in a corner. They had their swimming trunks on, but stood close together, silently. Solo felt old under their awestruck, respectful gaze. He lifted the bottle and swallowed. The liquid burned and choked him, until he bent over, expelling the third swallow forcibly over the feet of his companions.

"Watch it!" yelled Superkool.

Horse yanked the bottle away from Solo. Again it made the rounds, this time with less sputtering. They had settled into a grim ritual by the third round when three older boys walked in from the Basket Room.

The older boys shook their heads and smiled. "You dumb kids," one said indifferently as they began to dress.

Horse sat down on the bench, holding the bottle by the neck as if it were a dead chicken.

"Are you feeling it?" Zap asked excitedly. "I don't feel anything."

"I do," said Superkool, doing another wild little dance, pumping his hips in a way that made the others giggle.

Solo sat down beside Horse. He felt something all right. There had been a burning in his throat at first, but now he felt a dull throbbing in his stomach, a tightening there as if the whisky had jelled into a hot little ball. Was he going to be sick? He hoped desperately that he could hold it back. He mustn't get sick in front of the gang. He turned to see if the small kids were still watching, but luckily they had left. His eyes met those of an older boy.

"I bet you're feeling sick," the older boy said.

Solo tried to shrug.

The older boy pointed a warning finger at him. "You'll get caught!"

"So what?" Solo replied in a flat voice. His defiance surprised even himself and won approving glances from the gang.

"Yeah," said Zap. "So what!"

The older boy sneered and bent to tie his shoes.

Solo turned to Zap. "Give that here," he said and yanked the bottle away. Drinking until his eyes blurred, Solo jerked forward and struggled with a sudden roiling nausea.

"What a lush!" brayed Zap. "The guy can really drink. My old man can't do better."

Solo swallowed and swallowed, fighting to keep the nausea under control. He wished that he had passed up the last drink. His mouth filled with saliva, his eyes watered, and yet he felt good; he had proved himself to the guys. To the world! He was an outcast, like Mister Beck, and would always be in trouble. He didn't want to be a stockbroker like his father or a lawyer like the fathers of Horse and Superkool or anything stupidly respectable. He wanted to stand against the world. He wanted to see Bangkok, Kamakura, Singapore. He didn't care what happened.

"All right," he heard from behind his left ear. "What's going on?"

Solo glanced around; in the doorway to the Dressing Room stood the Basket Room attendant and Danny Richmond.

The tall lifeguard stepped forward and tore the nearly empty bottle from Zap's hand. Danny Richmond wore dark sunglasses, carried the tyrannical megaphone, and a silver whistle hung from a cord around his neck. Oil glistened on his prominent muscles. He regarded the bottle scornfully, then tossed it into a trash can.

"You kids be out of here in five minutes," he said in a voice so low that Solo could hardly hear it. "Five," Danny repeated. The dark glasses gave him the ominous look of a highway patrolman. He turned to leave, but turned back again. Leaning toward the quartet, he pointed the megaphone at each one—staying longest at Solo. "If any of you ever come into this pool again with something like that, I promise you you'll leave here in a squad car. I mean it. Now you get dressed and get the hell out!"

For a chilling moment he glared at Solo, then strode rapidly away with the Basket Room attendant at his heels.

The gang began snickering, but soon they were dressing as fast as they could. Solo knew that Danny Richmond had been easy on them because of his sister. If it hadn't been for the lifeguard's interest in her, the pool manager would be here by now and pretty soon the cops, who'd have hauled them down to the station. Then Solo would have had the fun of facing Sergeant Nolan. Well, let them put him in the state pen; he didn't care. As a matter of fact, he might like it.

❈ ❈ ❈

Eric was pedaling his bike in a wobbly pattern down the street. After leaving the pool, the guys had scattered in different directions, but all swore to meet at Larry's the next day.

Periodic waves of nausea swept through Eric, but he was past the worst of it. He was going to the garden and see Mister Beck. What the hell! He laughed out loud, feeling wonderfully old as he rode down the gray street. Glancing upward, he noticed that clouds were obscuring the sun; they lay across the town like a lumpy mattress. He had a bitter taste in his mouth; he felt sleepy; he felt the warm little ball in his stomach; but he kept on pedaling until Mister Beck's street appeared ahead. It occurred to him that he had never approached the garden except through the ravine, but then today everything was different. He giggled —couldn't help it—as the modest little houses wavered past his vision. He didn't recognize the Beck house on his first try. Coming back along the street, he then saw the driveway and the garage alongside a gray clapboard house. It looked so small and grim that he wondered how a man of the world like Mister Beck could stand to live there.

Walking his bike into the driveway, Eric realized how unsteady he really was; the tilting ground lurched up and met his feet. That didn't actually happen, but it felt as if it had. He giggled. Around the corner of the house he saw the chair, the weathered back of the old man's suntanned head. The garden had taken on a deep green hue beneath the clouds. It looked cozy, secret, inviting. Eric parked the bike inside the garage and trudged into the garden, almost reaching the chair before the bald head jerked around.

Mister Beck studied him briefly, then smiled. "Didn't think you were coming."

"Went to the pool," Eric said, flopping down at the old man's feet. He heard himself giggling.

"What's so funny?" Mister Beck asked, lips parted.

Eric did not answer for a few moments, because he could not stop giggling. "We got in dutch there," he finally said and rolled over on his stomach, resting his chin on both hands. He was giggling again. He had used the word "dutch," which was pretty funny. "Dutch" had been his grandfather's word for trouble. Until now Eric had never used it in his life. Mister Beck would know the word all right.

"What happened at the pool?" the old man asked sharply.

"Some guys I know—we were just messing around. Didn't do much." He heard himself snickering between words.

Mister Beck bent forward curiously. "Eric?"

Eric closed his eyes, wondering if that would help him to control the laughter. Everything was so funny. But then a kind of light moving under his eyelids made him feel sick.

He opened them and blinked as rapidly as he could.

"Eric?"

He knew if he looked directly at Mister Beck, he'd burst out laughing. So he stared at the ground.

"Eric, have you been drinking?"

"Yeah," he admitted, sitting up with a broad grin. "These guys, they bought a bottle from some kid. They had it at the pool, so we drank it in the Dressing Room." Eric smirked at Mister Beck. "This lifeguard threw us the hell out."

"I see," Mister Beck said quietly. "And then you came straight here. Is that right?"

"Yeah."

"Why?"

Eric shrugged, not understanding the question.

"Why come here?" the old man asked in a low voice.

Eric felt the laughter go out of his body.

"I am asking you, Eric, Why did you come here, drunk, to my garden?"

Eric heard the controlled fury then. He blinked, trying to find an answer. "I thought, I—"

"No," said Mister Beck. "You did not think. Or you thought *wrong.*" He leaned forward to utter in a low thrilling voice of anger, "How dare you come here in this condition?"

With difficulty Eric struggled to his feet.

"Out," hissed the old man. "Get out of here." His voice spiraled skyward in tight rage. "Get out of here! Get out! Get out, get out of here! Go on, you, get out of here!"

Eric found himself stumbling from the garden into the ravine. Then he was rolling, whipped by twigs and brambles until he came up hard against the trunk of a tree. He lay half curled against it, bruised and staring through the undergrowth at the pin oak visible above the garden, its top branches marking the southeast boundary of Mister Beck's world.

I won't ever see it again, Eric told himself.

He struggled to get his uncoordinated body into a sitting position against the tree. Never again—he wouldn't see it again. He felt a sob welling up in his throat like something alive. Never again—the garden—never again.

Getting to his feet, he tottered a moment, then careened down the hill, stumbling and falling twice before reaching the bottom. A tiny stream trickled through the gully. Wild ash, maple, and oak trees rose around him, so that when Eric stretched out alongside the stream, he could hardly see the sky through the branches. He lay there, listening to the lilting sound of the flowing water. Insects throbbed in the clump of woods. A bird warbled somewhere above his left ear. Everything moved around him until he felt like closing his eyes, and when he opened them again, rain was falling softly through the leaves, pelting his cheeks and lips. He raised his watch hand. It was time to go home. It was later than that—it was almost time for dinner. Not that he wanted any. He had been asleep—How long? At least an hour.

Rolling to one side, he regarded a thread of gray water between two banks not farther apart than the length of his hand. Raindrops were plunking lumpishly upon its slate surface. A few midges were circling in a soundless whirl above it. The rain fell like little pellets into the stream; the drops looked heavy when they burst, fruitlike, making a soft kind of music. The smell of green was overwhelming; it clung to the foggy air he took into his lungs. Above him the branches were swaying in a rhythm that nearly put him back to sleep. He lay for a lost time in the green smell and rainy music. He felt himself inside of something warm— held and rocked. Never in his life would he forget these secret moments when a green wet world held and rocked him to the whispery music of the rain. Never would he forget the thick earthy scent of something he could almost remember from somewhere else in another time. And never would he forget the terrible moments that abruptly followed. First, he felt a kind of strange restlessness within and then nausea collected in his gut like a burning fist that pushed cruelly upward.

Eric retched into the weeds. It felt as if his insides had been shoved clear out of his mouth. He had never vomited so explosively before.

Then he cried with his entire being. He cried for losing the garden, for losing Mister Beck. He cried for himself.

Meeting the Storm 🌿

Eric was confined to bed for the next three days with a very bad cold. Even though he had a fever during the first day, Mother could not hold back a lecture on the consequences of walking in the rain. He considered himself lucky that his parents had gone out to a party that night and had not been at home to witness his stumbling in, still half drunk. He had gone straight to bed, fending off Roddy's curiosity by claiming to be sick. And it was no pretense; he was sick all right. When Roddy clumped downstairs to eat the casserole left in the warming oven, Eric had slipped out of bed and brushed his teeth, then collapsed into bed again, awaking the next morning hot and cold and even sicker.

On the second day of his confinement, Susan came into his room and sat on the bed, staring thoughtfully at him like a nurse—or a judge.

"Danny told me," she began, "how you said hello to him for me. Thanks." After a pause she added without inflection, "He also told me what you and your friends did."

Eric met his sister's dark frown defiantly. There were

people who said she was pretty, but all he saw were the stony judgmental eyes, the set lips, the hard line of the jaw. For a long time he had known that he and Susan would never be friends, no matter how long they lived. Something had happened when they were little kids that he, and probably she, could not remember, and it would never be changed or forgiven by either of them. They'd be mortal enemies forever and not know why. But Eric knew this at least: He could never relent in his dealings with Susan, never concede or show weakness, or she'd crush him.

"Did you tell Mother?" he asked, meeting her eyes.

"No, as a matter of fact, I didn't. I just wanted you to know what Danny said. He said you better stay clear of those boys you were with."

"Are you going to tell Mother?"

Susan gave him a faint smile and got up.

"Are you?"

"Maybe." Susan put her hands on her hips. "Maybe not."

"If you don't tell Mother, I won't forget it."

"What does *that* mean?"

"I'll do you a favor, too."

Susan pursed her lips. "I won't tell her if you stop hanging around with those boys. I don't want you getting into more trouble. I don't want you ending up in the state reformatory or something and have people pointing me out as your sister. Understand?"

"Promise you won't tell her."

Susan walked to the door and turned. "I guess so."

"Promise."

"Promise," she muttered with a little dismissive shrug and left.

Eric stared at the rain falling steadily past the bedroom window. Even had he not broken off with Mister Beck, they couldn't be in the garden during such a rainy spell. He felt a sudden hope, then let it go. The old man would never allow him to set one foot in the garden again. Another kid would come along and take his place there. The likelihood of its happening brought Eric close to tears. He sucked in his lower lip and prayed to the air (because his family didn't practice religion) that the rain would continue until he was able to get out of bed.

The prayer was answered. The return of fair weather and the end of his confinement coincided. He could hardly wait to run through the gullies and climb the ravine into the garden. Not that he felt the old man would take him back, but he was prepared to beg for another chance. He'd get down on hands and knees and beg if it would do any good. He'd fight for a chance to be in the garden again, because throughout his confinement in bed, Eric had recalled the squares in which he had already sat, the stretch of lawn representing the squares yet to go. And he remembered lying next to the stream at the bottom of the gully, where something strange had happened to him, where the secret green world had enveloped him in a whispery music.

He had to get back to the garden.

Such thoughts were in his mind when he climbed the last step from the ravine and emerged on the flat sunlit lawn. There sat Mister Beck.

"You left your bike in the garage," the old man said promptly.

Eric approached, meeting the fierce blue eyes.

"Mister Beck," he said and halted. He cleared his throat to make his voice sound stronger. "I'm sorry for what I did. I apologize. I want to keep looking at the garden."

Mister Beck did not reply for a long time, but huddled in the chair with the shawl wrapped around his long scrawny neck. Eric was starting to lose hope, when the old man said abruptly, "All right, Eric, I accept your apology. You gave it like a man. Now I am going to tell you something. Ever since the other afternoon I have been asking myself, Why would Eric do such a thing? Why get drunk and take a chance of getting arrested? Why court more trouble than he already has, knowing it might lengthen his probation period or even result in the reformatory? Why would Eric be so self-destructive? And then it made sense. Eric, I wonder, did you want to be like me? A jailbird? Is that what you wanted?"

Eric thought hard. Had he really wanted to be like an old man? Well, not like any old man. But maybe like *this* old man. Come to think of it, it might be true. In a way. It really was.

"Yes," Eric admitted.

"That's kind of flattering. But, hell, you don't want to spend your life in prison. Now do you?" Mister Beck was smiling. "In a tiny cell?"

Eric smiled back. When he thought about it, it was stupid to want such a thing.

"Well, I'm glad you're back," said the old man. "The truth is, I missed you." Mister Beck thumped the arms of the chair hard. "So let's get on with the work." He was looking at the four strings staked out to make a square, half of which lay inside a flower bed.

Eric walked over to the square and said briskly, "I'm ready," and stepped inside.

※　※　※

Eric renewed his concentrating within the squares. He moved in slow methodical progression across the lawn, through the flower beds, into the territory of birdbath and tree. He and Mister Beck talked less than they previously had. During their lemonade breaks Eric was often busy, checking in one of his books the identity of a beetle that he might have seen in a previous square. And, of course, when he was sitting, not a word was exchanged between him and the old man. Often Mister Beck dozed, and sometimes Eric did not bother to stop sitting when the required hour had passed. This was especially true when he entered a square containing a tree, because there was so much then to occupy his attention. He studied the texture of the bark, the routes of foraging ants up and down the trunk, and from the limbs on which he often sat above his six-foot-square kingdom, Eric had an overview of the garden. In the shagbark hickory the squirrel they called Roger skittered to and fro, causing a frightful fuss, his red eyes regarding Eric with outrage for having trespassed.

The flower beds were also special worlds, and Eric was glad when his systematic progression through the garden brought him to one of them. He lay under a flower stalk, his cheek pressed against the pungent earth. He fixed his eyes at the entry of the green plant into the loam, allowing his mind to travel freely down into the earth along the twisting labyrinthine roots as if following nerves to the heart of the world. And sometimes he would conjure in his imagination the myriad grubs, the larvae, the worms, the countless tiny creatures squirming against the outstretched tentacles of the plant, moving like fish among the stolid coral branches in the blackest of oceans.

He noticed one afternoon that he could know the garden by smelling as well as looking at it. He sat cross-legged in a square and concentrated on the odors drifting toward him through the hot bright air. It was not easy, because his treacherous mind often played games, tricked him by wandering away from smells into thoughts. And yet after some practice he learned to sit with eyes closed and nostrils open, drawing into them a variety of smells that began to separate into distinct patterns, becoming as individual as a plant or an insect. He tried to discover the garden through sound, too, but soon give up this attempt, because to his disappointment most of the sounds entering the garden were from distant horns or from people calling across nearby yards or from jets whooshing overhead.

As he progressed from square to square, Eric began to feel with increasing wonder the throb of life everywhere in the garden. The lawn, the flower beds, the summer air itself, seemed to swell almost to bursting with things humming, whizzing, or crawling. And how often he saw things waiting motionlessly—to pounce, to attack. In one of his books Eric had read that no matter how small an animal is, there must always be a smaller one that will be eaten by it. And this was true. The garden seethed with silent murder, as everything alive moved toward its dinner. Within each square a new world was created, often with its own wildlife. For example, in the square next to the garage, under the morning glories, he found aphids, scale insects, and grubs.

In the square almost in the middle of the lawn, however, he found leafhoppers, blister beetles, and ladybugs. Each day he learned more about the insects, adding fact to fact until they formed a kind of web of knowledge. He understood the anatomical differences between a butterfly and a moth, between a locust and a katydid. He knew that the average insect can pull more than twenty times its own weight, whereas the average man—or horse, for that matter —cannot even pull the equivalent of its weight. And that was reason enough for him to watch a beetle trundling a clump of earth that in its eyes must have been the size of a truck.

Eric also got acquainted with animals that were just passing through, such as the tomcat who crept into the garden stalking young robins. He sometimes caught sight of a sleek blue racer, almost three feet long, slithering like a lively S repeating itself infinitely, bound for the ravine to hunt field mice. The brilliant sight of that blue reptile, a sinuous machine of destruction—at least for rodents—was enough to send him scurrying to the library for a book on snakes.

And he took out a book on weather, too, because he had learned that without understanding the weather he could not know the garden. The air above each square that he occupied had its own invisible but vital life. He learned to identify a change in air pressure by watching the flight of swallows across the garden; they skimmed the hedges in search of heavier air when the barometer was falling. He could tell from the change in sound that a storm front was approaching: everything was hollow and clear. He could also tell from the sudden release of odors in the garden; the more pungent it smelled, the lower the air pressure. He had this image of flower and grass breathing freer as the air loosened its grip on them.

Eric did not feel satisfied with sitting only in the full light of day. He came at sunset, oblivious to the gardening done by silent Miss Beck, and watched the sun go down like a hot coal, only to be replaced minutes later by the cold electric glow of fireflies hovering above the lawn. To explain his lateness getting home, Eric lied that he had gone to a long movie in the afternoon.

He came to the garden after midnight, too, when the family was asleep. Picking his way cautiously down the stairs from his room, Eric trotted along the dark streets and into the Beck driveway. He found the dim four lines of the string defining the square and stepped into the dark kingdom. He sat for a long time, never looking at his watch, but depending only upon the progress of the stars in their constellations, moving like spokes on an immense wheel across the night sky. When he saw the Northern Cross shift from a point directly overhead to the edge of the Beck roof (he had taken out a star book), Eric figured it was time to go home. And another time he got up very early—having set the timer on a wristwatch that was the best his father's money could buy—and crept out of the house again, arriving at the garden just before dawn. He sat in the cool dew and watched a faint blue light spread over the eastern sky above the houses across the ravine. Then a rich blush of orange began to seep above the pin oak and the shagbark hickory as if it were being slowly poured out of a bottle. And the whole sky seemed to quiver like something alive, shaking itself from sleep. He was still there in the dewy grass when, behind him, the screen door swung open and

Miss Beck came out to do her morning work. He did not turn to say hello, nor did she speak either, but he had an image of her in his mind—the tall rawboned woman with gunmetal-gray hair pulled back severely in a bun. He heard her quick footsteps going into the garage. He heard the snipping of shears in the flower bed behind his left shoulder. He imagined her working carefully, with the fastidious intent of someone who never laughed. Then it was time for him to go. Eric got up without looking back at the woman, without saying a word of good-bye, and trotted across the garden into the ravine. He ran home as fast he could through the glowing gullies afire with new light, and he reached home almost too late. Mounting the stairs, he heard Mother's alarm clock go off.

❊　❊　❊

And so he did each square. He became accustomed to the possibility of having different experiences in each of them, of liking some worlds better than others. But wherever he sat, something always happened. Always. He came to think of the garden not so much as a plot of ground anchored to the American landscape, but as part of the restless sea, immeasurable and surging without definite shape. Nothing was solid when he looked at it long enough. And everything breathed. Even the wood breathed. He would put his ear against the cottonwood and listen to its trunk give out varying sounds of life: creaking or groaning or sighing when a breeze roused it or the humidity changed.

Familiarity with the garden did not, however, make such easy work of looking at it. Each time he entered a square, it was like being an explorer in an uncharted land. At the finish of a day's sitting, Eric often found himself bathed in sweat, thoroughly exhausted, as if he had gone through some athletic paces with Silky.

And there were little dramas that daily took on importance in the garden. A neighborhood dog chased a rabbit across the lawn one afternoon, and for the rest of his life Eric would remember on the retina of his own eyes the flashing image of blue terror in the eye of the fleeing rabbit. And then one morning he discovered a dead robin at the base of the pin oak, its fuzz wet and sticky, already alive with maggots burrowing into the warm dead tissue. The bird must have fallen out of a nest high in the tree. The extraordinary thing was that neither he nor Mister Beck had known of a robin's nest up there. That had been a secret kept from them and sobered Eric with the realization that no matter how hard he looked or for how long, he would always miss something within these seventy-nine squares.

And then there was the mole. His presence in the garden was a major event, and had there been a newspaper to record everything that went on there, the mole would have drawn banner headlines.

Mister Beck, sitting in the chair, pointed a trembling finger at a zigzagging hump of earth that traveled midway across the lawn like the arrested wake of a dolphin through the green sea.

"Mole," he observed, grimacing. "That's the track of a mole."

Eric bent down and studied the hillock weaving across the lawn.

"Grubbing for worms," explained Mister Beck.

That day Eric sat in a square close to the mole track. He broke the rule about concentrating on things inside the square in which he sat. This day he stared beyond the white string at the wavering line of the small mound, unable to get that mole out of his mind. He could picture it under the earth, its soft fur easing through the moist loam, its big shovel-shaped feet digging relentlessly away, its dirt-caked snout wiggling rapidly to sense out the presence of escaping worms.

The mole was a ravenous invader, a bulldozer of death, wreaking havoc among the grubs and worms and other subterranean life. Eric could imagine it breaking into a tiny creature's home and scooping up a soft little body into its red mouth.

"I once heard somewhere," Mister Beck remarked later as they sipped lemonade in the sun-washed garden, "if a mole's deprived of food for only half a day, it will starve to death."

"Let it," Eric said grimly to himself, not in hatred of the mole, but in defense of the underground of the garden.

꽃 꽃 꽃

It was a Thursday, a day scheduled for his probation interview at the police station. The prospect did not put him into a cheery mood, especially when the garden was there waiting for him. It was going to be warm and humid, the sort of weather that encourages the insects to emerge from their secret places in droves, all glistening and tremulous and busy.

As Eric dressed in a mixed mood—going slowly to avoid the station at one moment and dressing faster to get to the garden at the next—his brother, Roddy, was fooling around on the bedroom floor with a dump truck and some plastic

German infantrymen. He had a sore throat and could not go to the ball park.

Roddy glanced up while Eric was tying his shoes. "Hey," Roddy said, "how about hitting me a few fly balls?"

Eric pulled the knot tight and replied indifferently, "You better stay inside, if you're sick."

"I told you, I'm not sick."

Eric yawned and rubbed his eyes. He had stayed up long past midnight, reading about snakes.

"It's just a sore throat."

Eric picked up the book from his bed and shoved it between his jeans and stomach, intending to read between sittings in the garden. He had fallen asleep in the middle of Western Diamondback Rattlesnake.

"Hey, what are you doing?" Roddy asked, holding a German soldier in his fist.

"I got to get going," said Eric. "You already ate breakfast, didn't you? Or I'll make you some toast and leave it."

"Sure I had breakfast. Where are you going now?" Roddy threw the soldier down in exasperation. "At least you could hit me a couple of fly balls."

Eric turned at the door and glanced at his dejected brother. "Another time. Okay?"

"But you won't. You're always . . . going somewhere. I mean"—Roddy searched for a better description of Eric's bizarre behavior—"you never watch TV anymore."

"Listen, get rid of that sore throat. Okay?" And Eric strode briskly toward the stairs.

At his back he heard Roddy's high-pitched pleading voice, "Ah, come on. Hit me a couple of fly balls, will you? It won't take long!"

"I can't," Eric yelled while taking the stairs fast. He felt guilty for denying Roddy such a small thing, such a little time, but the garden was there waiting, and before the garden he had that disagreeable interview at the police station. He had a momentary glimpse of Father's world— the busy, demanding schedule that excluded the desires of people who had fewer responsibilities.

While he was buttering a piece of toast, the phone rang. Eric picked up the kitchen phone and heard a voice vaguely familiar: low in tone, precise in its enunciation, the voice of someone guarded and fastidious.

It was Miss Beck.

She politely asked him to drop by The Lonely Hunter "at his convenience," but didn't tell him why.

This request troubled him all the way to the police station. He'd rather face Sergeant Nolan than Miss Beck, although the reason for this feeling was not clear. Or it was in a way. Because somehow Miss Beck had the power to stand between him and Mister Beck, between the two of them and the garden. The woman was like an adult conscience coming into a game designed for guys his own age. She was an intruder who might influence Mister Beck just when everything was going so well in the garden. Eric was sure that Miss Beck hated him, and by the time he entered the police station, he felt a strong resentment of the woman even before their meeting at The Lonely Hunter.

꙰ ꙰ ꙰

Looking steadily at the sergeant, Eric denied having seen Mister Beck again.

Nolan regarded him closely. "I'm glad to hear it. One thing we don't need is you kids hanging around a guy like Beck." He swiveled the chair to face another officer. "Am I right?"

"You said it," replied the officer.

Neither of them had their usual bantering air in dealing with Eric. He realized they were serious.

"Don't worry," he said vaguely. "I'm doing okay."

Coming out of the police station, Eric saw Bones heading for it. Eric stopped, but tall and gangly Bones continued on, yelling over his shoulder, "Hey, we're not supposed to talk to each other!" And then he waved gaily and called, "Everyone wonders where you've been hanging out lately!"

"Everyone" meant the gang. It occurred to Eric that he hadn't met the gang in days—three, maybe four. Now and then he had thought of them; frequently he had meant to go to Larry's, but somehow he got sidetracked. By the garden, by his reading. It was as if he had a full-time job with no room in his schedule for the gang. Whatever the reason for his absence, the gang would demand an explanation, sooner or later. As he biked toward The Lonely Hunter, he had a frightening image of Horse backing him against the wall with that hammerlike motion of a poking finger, demanding to know where he had been and why he had deserted the guys.

Then he was at the entrance of the little gift shop. Squinting up at the sign, THE LONELY HUNTER, he took a deep breath and opened the door; overhead a bell tinkled, causing the gray-haired woman behind the counter to look up from an open account book.

At his initial sight of Miss Beck, he felt a sudden relief.

There was an aura of calm about the woman that dispelled his fear of an unpleasant confrontation. Not that she smiled at him; she did not. But there was no grimace, no aggressive stance, no glowering like that of a math teacher he'd had a couple of years ago.

And yet as he approached the counter, abruptly she put both hands on it in a gesture of defense, of protection, that gave him to understand how alike they were—each fearing the other. Eric stopped before getting there and rested his hip against a display table.

Neither had spoken a word, yet he felt as though they had been facing each other for minutes. From somewhere behind a glass cabinet containing all sorts of china came the heavy metronomic sound of a clock. The silence otherwise was almost palpable, as much of a presence as all the objects for sale in the shop. The room felt peopled, an audience for him and this strange calm woman.

Then she began speaking of her father in a low, re-strained voice. Evidently she assumed that Eric knew about the prison term, because it was taken for granted in her explanation: how he had gone to prison when she was only eleven years old; how at first she had hated him for his crime and had resolved never to visit him; how at last, when she was almost twenty years old, she had gone to the prison and seen him. "I can't explain my feelings to you, Eric," said Miss Beck. "It wasn't that I forgave my father. I did not. I never did and never will. But I had learned to live with the fact of his crime and his terrible life. Because he suffered, I suppose, as much as a human being can suffer for a mistake so awful, so utterly final, that nothing can ever make up for it." Miss Beck paused, and Eric knew why; she was waiting for the question he then asked in a voice so small he could hardly recognize it as his own.

"What did Mister Beck do?"

"He committed murder, Eric," the woman replied without inflection, without hesitation. "I never saw him for so many years because of what he'd done." Miss Beck said the words slowly, as if remembering in some way those years between eleven and twenty. "Then his sister, my aunt—she's dead now—told me how he was suffering for what he had done. That's what decided me to go visit him—not forgiveness, but pity. I could never forgive him, never," the woman claimed in a voice of sudden force, "but I understood at last what he was suffering. From that first prison meeting, I kept seeing him each visiting day for almost thirty years. And then a few months ago he was paroled. Eric, do you have any idea why I'm telling you all this?"

"Because—I'm Mister Beck's friend."

"Because of that and because it won't be a secret much longer in a town this size that my father was serving a life sentence for murder. I didn't want you to be caught unawares."

"He would have told me," Eric maintained.

"He might have told you, but it's not a very easy thing to tell anyone. Even a good friend."

"He would have told me."

Miss Beck sighed deeply, and for the first time since Eric had entered the shop, she removed her hands from the counter and gripped them together, kneading the knuckles. "There's something else," she said. "They paroled him because for all those years he had been a model prisoner. And because he is going to die."

No sooner had Eric heard those last words than he felt himself trembling. It was as if he had been lowered suddenly into a vat of ice water. He couldn't stop the sensation of trembling in his arms and legs.

"You see, Eric," the woman continued in her low calm voice, which he knew must be costing her a great effort to control, "when I brought him home with me, I figured it was the least I could do as his daughter. He has suffered beyond anyone's ability to imagine it. But I knew what was in store for us eventually. Someone would remember—perhaps a news photo. A leak from the prison. It's bound to happen. And I was prepared. Then"—she looked almost with tenderness at Eric, surely with sadness—"you came along. I didn't want it to happen, this friendship, because even though he obviously enjoys it, I had no idea what sort of boy you would be. How you'd react when you found out."

Eric glanced around the shop, trying to blink back the tears. All he could think of was Mister Beck getting out of prison only to die. It wasn't fair. It wasn't fair. Eric felt his fists tightening at his sides. He was angry, but not at Miss Beck or the prison officials or anyone. He was angry because it wasn't fair for Mister Beck to spend a lifetime in prison and then to get out only to die.

"I don't want him to die," Eric said gravely. He added with a sudden touch of anger, "I hate it." His eyes were brimming; he hated that, too. "Does he know it, too?" Eric asked, appalled at the thought.

"Yes, Eric, he does."

In yet another silence he heard the clock ticking like a thickly pulsing heart. It thudded hypnotically. He was look-

ing everywhere in the shop except at Miss Beck. Then
finally he found the courage again to look at her without
breaking into tears. "Does he know you were going to tell
me today?"

"I thought if anyone tells him you know so much about
him, it should be you."

"Why me?" asked Eric, feeling a tremor of fear. "I don't
want to talk about—all that. Why should I?"

"Because you say you're his friend. If you can't discuss
something this important with him, then you better wonder
how deep your friendship goes."

The other thought struck him, the one lurking behind the
thought of Mister Beck dying. "Did he really—kill someone?" Eric asked as if needing that idea confirmed yet
again.

Miss Beck nodded and turned away. She bent over some
plates stacked on a shelf behind the counter, rubbing at one
with a handkerchief. Eric realized that she, too, was close
to tears, that she was someone who always wanted to be in
control of herself, and so rather than embarrass her by
seeing that control go to pieces, Eric turned without another word and walked out.

Where should he go? He asked himself after climbing on
his bike and pedaling away.

Where? To the garden and to see Mister Beck? That was
a meeting he had better put off until he could hold in his
mind those two terrible ideas: Mister Beck was a murderer;
Mister Beck was dying.

Should he go to Larry's and see the gang? He couldn't
listen to their jokes and roughhouse with them while Mister
Beck was on his mind. Go home and read? No book in the

world could hold his attention today. Swimming? A movie? Where should he go?

But already he had pointed the bike in the direction of the Beck house. Miss Beck was right. Between friends certain things had to be faced.

❊ ❊ ❊

It was almost noon when Eric entered the garden. From all sides he heard the singing of birds, and overhead, little puffs of cloud sailed past other clouds as towering and solid as mountains. His spirits lifted, even though he hated and feared the coming interview. It was the garden itself that made him feel good. It was as if nothing that happened within it, even between him and Mister Beck, could destroy what was good there: the green things, the insects and birds, even the clouds overhead.

"Thought you weren't going to make it today," Mister Beck said, waving from his chair near the birdbath.

Eric approached hesitantly. What should he do? Should he come out with it? He met the steady questioning gaze of the blue eyes.

"I was sort of afraid to come," he said.

"What's wrong?" Then after a short pause Mister Beck added quietly, "More about me?"

Eric nodded.

The old man folded his hands in a gesture of resignation. "How did you find out?"

"Miss Beck told me at the shop."

"Did she tell you everything?" Mister Beck squinted at him thoughtfully. "She told you what I did to go to prison?"

"Yes, sir," Eric said. This was the first time he had used that term of respect with Mister Beck. But now it was appropriate because a little formality might enable them to talk easier of intimate things.

"I wonder if she told you the whole story," Mister Beck mused. The taut look on his old face suggested an inner struggle. "I wonder," he said softly, as if hardly believing his own words, "if she told you it was her own mother I killed."

Before Eric had time to assimilate that incredible revelation, Mister Beck thumped the chair arms hard in a characteristic gesture of decision. "Sit down, Eric. I have things to tell you."

Eric sat down near the old man's feet. He did not look at Mister Beck, but kept his gaze fixed on the garden, on grass and trees and flowers. It was as if the garden could hold him in the real world while an old voice coming out of the noontime light spoke of love and hate and violence in a world long past before he was even born.

Mister Beck began simply enough by speaking again of life at sea. It had been a good life for a young man without any goal, but there came a time when he had wanted more security. So he had quit the sea, and by persuading some businessmen to provide him with financial backing, Mister Beck had gone into the pleasure-boat business here in this state. That had been more than half a century ago. His hunch had been a good one; rich people discovered they could play sailor on inland waters as well as on the ocean. Soon the cabin cruisers built by Mister Beck were plying rivers and lakes throughout the Midwest. Money rolled in; within a few years he had become a wealthy young man.

"About that time I met a girl and fell in love," continued Mister Beck. "What do you know about love, Eric?"

"Enough, I guess." Eric was thinking of his sister and her gawking boyfriends. If that was love, he hoped to escape it.

"Enough?" Mister Beck laughed briefly. "No one ever knows enough about love. But, anyway, this girl and I got married, and we were happy. And we had Sophia. Sophia —that's my daughter."

This was the first time Eric had heard Miss Beck's first name. It was soft and lovely and didn't seem to fit her.

Mister Beck was talking then about his married life. A kind of dreamlike quality entered his voice, as if the old man could no longer believe that he was describing happiness that he himself had felt. His business had thrived. His wife had been a loving mother to Sophia, who had been such a spirited little girl, full of pranks and laughter.

"Maybe I had more than a man can rightfully expect from life," said Mister Beck sadly. "Because you see, Eric, my wife found another man she loved more than me." There was a wavering in the old voice that made Eric glad he was looking at the garden, not at Mister Beck. "I couldn't accept it. Do you understand?"

"Did she tell you about this—man?"

"No, but I found out."

"If you didn't get along," said Eric softly, "couldn't you get a divorce?"

"They weren't so common in those days. But, of course, I could have gotten one. I just didn't want to. And we did get along, in our way. I wanted her, Eric. I wanted to keep trying until she came back to me of her own free will."

"Did you tell her?"

"Ah, that's the question. I see you understand a good deal, Eric. No, I didn't tell her. She never knew I was aware of the other man. If I'd told her, if we'd sat down and discussed it, perhaps things might have ended differently. Oh, God, if only they had"—the old voice broke momentarily.

Eric stared at a bed of phlox; a cloud of bees undulated above the flowers like a veil moved by a gust of wind. And then he relaxed a little when the old voice spoke again, with its characteristic strength.

"Eric, I can't explain jealousy to you except to say it's like a fire out of control. Consumes everything. I let it consume everything good my wife and I had had together. And when I burned up every wonderful memory, I began to hate her. At all hours of the day I imagined her with the other man. I hated them both. It was all I really lived for, this jealousy that had burned out of me all reason, all love, all understanding. I forgot about Sophia. I forgot about the woman my wife had once been. And so one afternoon I left work in the middle of a sales meeting and drove home as fast as I could, dreading what I might find there, but almost sure I knew what I would find. And my worst fear was realized. They were in the bedroom; I heard them"—Mister Beck's voice rose to a high chilling coil of sound. "There was a gun cabinet in the study. I went in there and wrenched a gun out and kicked the door in and shot. I emptied both barrels—"

Eric yanked out some tufts of grass fiercely and mauled the blades in his trembling fingers.

Birdsong invaded the garden with sudden raucous sound, as if everything alive in the seventy-nine squares had been listening to the story along with Eric and with the terrible climax could no longer remain still.

He shredded each blade scrupulously. The bruised grass became dark and wet.

"Eric?"

He kept crushing the blades of grass.

"What I did hurts you, doesn't it?" the old man said gently. "It may help you to know that for the last forty years, for every day of that forty years, I have regretted what I did, I have wished—how desperately I've wished—I could relive that one afternoon. How many times in memory I've pulled that trigger, how many countless times I've wished to be back there at the gun cabinet, so I could put the gun in place and leave the house. Eric, I will suffer for what I did as long as I draw breath."

Eric continued to shred the grass brutally.

"Is there something else?" asked Mister Beck.

At last Eric glanced up, squinting at the dark outline of the old head against the glare of sunlight. "Miss Beck said they let you out of prison to die."

Mister Beck nodded without hesitation. "That's right."

Eric stared into the blinding sunlight at a face he could not see.

"Is it that you want to know how long I have?" Mister Beck asked quietly.

"Yes, sir."

"Well, there's no way of knowing that." The old man pursed his lips judiciously. "Let's just say this is probably our only summer together."

Eric yanked out a fresh bunch of grass. "I hate it," he muttered.

"There's no sense hating it. The thing is get on with what we have to do here in the garden." The old man pointed at four pegs with white string taut between them.

"I don't know if I can do it right now," said Eric.

"I can understand that," replied Mister Beck in a voice almost tender. "But what you've learned about me today, you'll still know tomorrow. Whereas the square is waiting. It's time to sit in that square."

Eric got slowly to his feet and stepped inside the square. At first he could think of nothing but Mister Beck. But he kept trying to shift his attention to the square, as the old man wanted him to do, and after a while he succeeded. Only after he had completed the square did all the terrible facts rush into his consciousness again. Yet after a glass of lemonade, during which break he and Mister Beck did not exchange more than a few comments about the weather— tactily acknowledging their conversation had ended for the day—Eric pulled the pegs and stretched them to encompass a new square in which he also sat. When he had finished, he saw that the old man had fallen asleep. Usually he let Mister Beck doze, but today it was necessary for him to declare something. Gently he shook the frail old shoulder.

Mister Beck awakened with a start. His blue eyes took a few moments to focus on Eric; spittle gleamed on his thin lips.

"I just wanted to say I'm going now." Eric had not taken his hand from the bony shoulder. "I'll be here tomorrow."

"Good," Mister Beck murmured with a contented smile and fell almost instantly back to sleep.

※　※　※

Each member of the family attacked the casserole according to his individual method: Eric and Roddy with directness and speed; Susan with finicky caution; Father with methodical accuracy; Mother with brooding sporadic energy. It was a quiet dinner, however, with a strange atmosphere of tension that made Eric wonder. Mother was unusually silent. Most of the time she led the conversation during mealtimes, either by describing her own varied activities or questioning the rest of the family about theirs. Tonight the air was filled with little more than the sound of forks and knives clicking against plates. And Eric noticed that both his parents were glancing thoughtfully at him, whereas Susan sat with her lipsticked mouth slightly parted as if in anticipation and Roddy resolutely avoided all eye contact with him.

Something was up, all right. Eric waited, but nothing happened. Then, after dinner, he strolled into the family room where Father had already turned on the television. Roddy did not come into the room, which in its own way was significant; that kid never missed an opportunity to stare at the tube. Finally Mother did come in and sit down; this was also out of the ordinary, since it was her usual practice after dinner to work on her committee reports in the study.

So here he was, sandwiched between his parents on the couch, facing one of those situation comedies that lean on canned laughter and lack of communication.

And then it came.

Mother said without warning, "You have been seeing him, Eric."

He turned to look at her face; her forehead was streaked with ghostly reflected light from the television set. "Who?"

"People are not as stupid as you may think," she said hotly.

"Your mother," put in Father from Eric's other side, "means the old man."

"The murderer," added Mother.

"Don't call him that," said Eric.

"Oh, I'll call him exactly what he is," replied Mother, getting to her feet and blocking his view of the television.

He stared up at her silhouette against a background of roiling color from the set. "Do you know you're consorting with a convicted murderer, Eric?"

Father leaped to his feet and threw the wall switch, flooding the room with light.

Eric didn't like this; he felt as though his parents had trapped him in the family room, whereas they could have spoken out at dinner.

"I heard about him today," continued Mother, pacing up and down, kneading her fingers. "Not only a convict but a murderer." She halted and leaned toward Eric. "Did you know that?"

Eric set his jaw.

"From the look on your face I'd say you did know that. Well?" When Eric still didn't reply, she appealed to Father. "Ralph, speak to him."

"Eric," said Father.

Eric turned sullenly to look at Father, who had taken a seat beside him again on the couch.

"The point is not what you know about Mister Beck. The point is, you must stop seeing him."

"He's only an old man," Eric argued.

"That is not how society sees it. Murder is the one thing

a man can commit and never live down. Never. That's the way it is, Eric, and you can't change it."

"I'm not trying to change anything."

"The point is," Father persisted, "you must stop seeing him."

"No," said Eric.

He watched his parents exchange glances of shock and worry. When he had broken the school windows, they had not seemed this upset.

Mother sat down and impulsively took his hand in hers.

"Can't you see how wrong you are?" she asked in a pleading voice. "Spending your time with a man the whole town will soon know is a murderer?"

"Was a murderer," corrected Eric. "He's not a murderer now."

"Don't mince words with me."

"He paid for what he did. They paroled him."

"Yes, they did," Mother said quietly. "Because he is dying."

They knew that much: Did they know all of it? Eric wondered in panic. Did they know that Mister Beck was the murderer of his own wife?

"What Mister Beck is now," put in Father, taking up the argument, "has little relevance to your situation, son. We're concerned with your probation. I don't think the police would deal kindly with you if they learned you went against orders and spent time with such a man."

With a parent on each side of him and the television barraging him with people racing around and periodic laughter, Eric couldn't think. So he just said, "Mister Beck is my friend."

"What does that mean?" Mother asked anxiously.

"I can't let him down."

Father rose and turned off the television. Silence swept into the room like a fresh breeze.

Parents and son remained a long time in silence.

"If you persist," Father began at last, "we'll have to take your privileges away."

"Allowance, everything," added Mother.

Eric was staring at his dirt-stained hands. Soap and water could not remove all the dirt from the creases. He was proud to have such hands because they belonged to the garden.

"Are you listening!" cried Mother.

Eric looked at her, appalled to see such fear and rage in her face. "I'm sorry," he said.

"Does that mean you promise never to see him again?" asked Mother eagerly.

"No."

"I can't believe this is happening, Ralph," Mother said, rising and pacing again.

"You are taking a big chance, Eric," said Father gravely. "We can keep you inside this house."

"I'll get out," Eric muttered, not looking at either of them.

"I can't believe this," said Mother, pacing.

Eric felt sorry for her. Mother was usually so brisk and optimistic; even when he had been placed on probation, she had held up and declared at dinner one night that maybe it was all for the best, that they would all learn something valuable from Eric's probation. To see her so worried and vulnerable went through him like a knife. But he would not relent.

"I don't want to cause trouble," he said, "but Mister Beck is my friend. I can't let him down."

"Can you possibly give me one good reason," Mother said, halting in her tracks, "why you must continue seeing him?"

Eric met her eyes steadily. "Because he's dying. I'm his only friend. How can I let him down now?"

He watched his parents again exchange glances, only this time their faces had new expressions—softer, bewildered, thoughtful.

"When you put it that way," Father said after a long pause, "maybe we can"— Father looked again at Mother, whose eyes told him something—"let matters stand as they are."

"For the present," Mother added. "But you must be careful, Eric."

"About what?"

"Telling your other friends about him."

"What your mother means," put in Father, "is the harm your friendship could do you if the town ever found out about Mister Beck's past."

"And sooner or later everyone will find out," declared Mother tremulously.

"But for right now," said Father with a sigh, "you can see him."

"Thank you both," Eric said in a voice thick with emotion, and left.

※   ※   ※

When he entered the bedroom, his brother gave him a sidelong glance of apprehension.

Eric undressed and climbed into bed, holding his book about snakes. Roddy had flicked off his own bedside light and pulled the sheet up to his chin and faced the wall.

"Why did you do it?" Eric asked.

There was no reply.

"I know you told them. But why?"

"Mother said she wouldn't tell you," Roddy murmured sullenly.

"Mother said nothing. It wasn't very hard to figure out who squealed. When was it you followed me?" After a long silence Eric added, "Come on, tell me. I'm just curious. I won't hit you."

Roddy mumbled something.

"What was that?" asked Eric.

"Couple days ago."

"What did you see?"

"You and that old man," Roddy started, and paused, testing Eric's control. Then he continued: He had seen Eric sitting in the square and drinking lemonade with that old man who never left his chair.

"Is that what you told Mother?"

"I just told her I saw you and him."

Good, thought Eric. He was glad that Roddy hadn't mentioned the squares, because explaining it might have had an adverse effect on his parents. They might think it was all crazy and again deny him permission to see Mister Beck.

"What did you think I was doing there?" Eric asked cautiously.

"How should I know?" said Roddy, still facing the wall. "You were playing some kind of game, I guess." Roddy turned then and looked at Eric from small bright eyes. "The thing is, you aren't supposed to see that old man."

"Why did you tell on me? That's what I want to know."

Roddy raised himself on one elbow. "You never tell me anything anymore."

"What am I supposed to tell you?"

"I don't know. You—" Roddy searched for an explanation of his discontent. "You act like I'm not here."

"I'm sorry. I didn't mean to."

The apology emboldened Roddy to say more. "You used to play with me. Now you don't. You don't even say anything. You just get dressed and leave, or like when you're here, you read those books."

"Okay, I understand. From now on I'll try to make it up to you. Roddy?"

"Yeah?" Roddy had turned back to the wall.

"I know you're here," Eric said. "It's just that I have a lot of things on my mind."

Roddy turned his head thoughtfully, then smiled. "Okay," he said.

Later, when the room was dark and he could hear his brother breathing rhythmically in sleep, Eric kept thinking about Mister Beck. Mister Beck had spent forty years in prison for murdering his own wife. That was the kind of thing Eric could see in the movies and on television, but he hadn't expected to meet up with it in real life. In real life it was different; in real life a killer took real lives. Mister Beck had really killed a woman. That made him someone who must always be a stranger, because Eric could never share such knowledge with him. Not really. There would be that gulf between them—this sense of having taken a life.

And yet Eric felt closer to Mister Beck than to anyone

else. He could not give the old man up, no matter what happened. Because nobody could stop him from being the old man's friend. Nobody. Not the police, not his parents, not the gang.

Nobody.

☙ ☙ ☙

There was only a third of the garden left to go. Eric had sat his way through two thirds of it, one six-foot square after another, in a slow but relentless process across lawn and flower bed, like a snail.

Every morning Eric set out from home as though to work, and the family watched him leave without comment.

One morning on his way through the back ravines, Eric found himself abruptly surrounded by birds. They were around him without warning, converging almost magically out of the air. They hopped and twittered on the ground, through bushes, among tree limbs, seeming to boil with energy as their chirping and singing reached a crescendo. It was a very strange moment. Eric felt that if he knew more about birds, he might understand what had just happened; because in a way those birds had been telling him something. He meant to discuss this with Mister Beck, but forgot about it when he reached the garden and saw, leaning against the side of the house, about a dozen canvases, all painted, with the old man seated in front of them, smiling.

"Come here!" Mister Beck called gaily. "I had Sophia bring them out before leaving. This is some of my prison painting."

Eric stared cautiously at the leaning canvases.

"Come on, take a good look!"

Eric smiled politely, walked up to the first painting, knelt, and examined it. What he saw was a couple of prisoners in striped suits lounging against a wall, except that he had to concentrate a long time before actually seeing those men, because at first they seemed like part of the wall; the bumpy swirls of paint served both for their flesh and for the wall itself. And their faces were a kind of purple, a color almost identical to that of the wall, also. And nothing was happening either: just two prisoners leaning against a blank wall that was the same color and texture as they were.

"The exercise yard," explained Mister Beck, with a hint of pride. "Next to cell block D."

Eric nodded with an uneasy smile, then knelt beside the next painting. At first it looked like confusing lines—also a kind of purple—but eventually he realized that two hands were gripping some prison bars. The painting was of two hands; that's all. And so it went down the line of canvases. Most of them were gray or purple or brown, but all contained people, or at least parts of people, that Eric couldn't recognize without concentrating very hard, and even when he could distinguish between people and walls or corridors, they didn't remind him of people in real life. They looked like something from a nightmare. The truth was, the paintings only made him feel uncomfortable.

Kneeling in front of the last one, Eric pretended to study it a long time. He was postponing the moment when he knew he must comment on the paintings. What could he say?

"Well?" said Mister Beck impatiently when at last he stood up.

"I don't know much about art," Eric said, hoping that this evasive remark would suffice.

But Mister Beck persisted. "Well?"

"They make me feel"—Eric struggled to be honest—"kind of funny."

"Funny?"

"Like uneasy."

"Good," said Mister Beck, sitting back. "That's what they make me feel, too."

Relieved by the old man's reaction, Eric slipped his hands into his pockets and glanced at the garden.

"Ready to begin?" Mister Beck asked.

Eric shook his head. "I wouldn't concentrate."

"Why not?"

Eric squinted judiciously at the sky. Mare's-tail clouds were spreading in stringy white wisps across the blue. "Pressure's changing," he observed.

"Yeah?" Mister Beck scratched his bald head. "What has air pressure got to do with your ability to concentrate?"

"When the pressure drops, it's hard to concentrate," Eric said. He went on to explain that the lower the pressure, the less oxygen is forced into the lungs, causing people to suffer from lack of oxygen and therefore to feel edgy, restless, unable to concentrate.

Mister Beck snorted. "You sound like a professor." Then he smiled broadly. "I hope that doesn't insult you."

But Eric wasn't listening to the old man's banter. A quartet of swallows were swooping low over the bushes of the next yard. "See how low they are?" Eric said. "That way they can use the heavier air near the ground for flying." Again he studied the sky in which cobwebby clouds were beginning to appear in the northwest. "Going to rain," he announced.

Mister Beck followed his gaze. "Rain? Not many clouds that I can see. Are you sure?"

"Yes," Eric said. "I am."

Mister Beck looked at the sky, almost devoid of clouds except for a few wispy ones gliding over the northwest corner of the house, and then he looked at the boy. "Okay," the old man said after a long pause. "I believe you, I guess. So we'd better get the paintings inside the house."

Eric handled them with great care, even though he didn't like them. By the time he had stacked all of them against a kitchen wall, a cloud mass was forming over the roof.

Mister Beck, still in his chair in the garden, was studying it. "I'll be damned," he said with a touch of surprise. "You may be right at that."

"It'll rain pretty soon," Eric declared.

"Then get me inside, too."

Eric hadn't expected this request for help from Mister Beck. Until now the old man had asked only for his cane when he needed to go inside the house. He'd wobble on the cane, but make it by himself—or make it most of the way. And if Eric had to help, he did not accept the help cheerfully; he grumbled or cursed. Not until this moment had he ever acknowledged any need at the outset. So with apprehension and sadness Eric helped him to his feet and steadied him with difficulty. Mister Beck let him slip an arm around that bony waist and do most of the work. It occurred to Eric that until their recent talk about the state of Mister Beck's health, the old man had felt obliged to appear stronger than he really was. Now Mister Beck could accept help without faking. So it was probably a good thing, Eric thought, that the idea of death had been brought into the open. It was okay, especially because he did not really believe this was their last summer together.

As Eric helped the old man into the house, the anvil top of a dark storm cloud started to spread overhead. Mister Beck hesitated in the doorway and glanced up, smiling.

When Mister Beck reached the living room, he let go of Eric's arm and slumped wearily down on a couch. Eric sat opposite him in that dim gloomy room with too much heavy furniture in it. There was an airy bright quality about Miss Beck's gift shop that she didn't bring to her own house. Here it was stuffy and somber, as though it had been lifted out of the last century. Eric decided that if the daughter belonged here, the father did not; old and shriveled though he was, nearly lost in the brown upholstery of the couch, Mister Beck belonged somewhere uncrowded, with large windows letting the sunlight in, and long white drapes fluttering in the breeze coming from the ocean on which he had sailed adventurously as a young man.

The room got suddenly darker. Through the window Eric noticed some tree limbs bending almost parallel to the street. "Pretty soon now," he said with pride in his assessment of the rain.

"I believe you," Mister Beck said with conviction.

"Sir, I'd like to go out in it."

"What?"

"When the rain comes, I'd like to be in the garden."

Mister Beck laughed. "Then go."

❧ ❧ ❧

Eric rushed from the house into the garden. A few birds were cheeping in the hickory tree, getting themselves wedged down to ride out the coming storm.

Seeing them up there, Eric realized at last why there had been so many birds congregating this morning in the ravine. They had anticipated the storm long before a cloud had appeared in the sky. Eric took a few steps into the garden and halted. Birds in the cottonwood and maple were chirping irritably. Their cries seemed extraordinarily clear, as if coming through a long corridor; the clouds, solid overhead, were acting like a sounding board.

Then the birds became silent.

There wasn't one sound in the air except that of a rush of wind. Everything alive was huddled down, waiting.

Eric, studying the pin oak's fine breadth of sturdy limb, decided to meet the storm from there. He climbed with difficulty to the first branch high above the ground, then scrambled with ease midway up the tree and straddled a thick limb while holding onto an overhead branch with one hand and bracing himself against the trunk with the other. He felt secure, as adapted to the shape of the tree as the birds were. He was certain that it would be a swift but violent storm. He had felt it in his bones ever since the first few strands of cirrus clouds drifted overhead. Just as the initial raindrops fell, Eric knew there was nothing about this garden and sky above it that he didn't know. He shouldn't be in a tree during an electrical storm, but he couldn't give up these moments here in the pin oak. He watched some sparrows sitting puffed and motionless on a branch nearby. They cheeped faintly when the rain began cascading over their ruffled feathers. He felt like one of them. He took a deep breath and felt his sides billow out like theirs; he held his elbows close in as though they were wings. The rain streaming down his face soaked into his feathers.

A flash, a roll.

The quickening downpour spun the dark green leaves of the oak tree, flipping their smooth pale undersides to glisten momentarily like twisting foil.

Another flash of lightning. A following roll of thunder.

Eric waited for the next flash, even as the rain slanted obliquely in at him through the leaves, pelting his face coolly, fiercely. The flash came. Glancing at his watch he counted one, two, three seconds before the thunderclap followed. Three times one fifth—sound traveling one fifth of a mile per second—and he'd have the approximate distance of the lightning bolt from the garden. He knew that. Six tenths of a mile—more than a half mile away. He had calculated it. His knowledge of the distance of the lightning away from the garden put him in closer touch with the progress of the storm. The lightning was something recognizable, like that blue racer in the garden slithering toward a feast of field mice in the ravine. Like a spider hastening along one of its threads to pounce on a trapped fly. Like a mantis. Like a robin pulling a worm out of the lawn. The storm was coming with tremendous irresistible force, driving the sturdy privet into scattered shapes, flattening the grass, hammering the pliable stalks of flowers into the ground. He felt the tree shaking around him like a living animal; it had a pulse, a beating heart at its core. It held him like a fist, and he moved with its wild motion as if it had been a horse galloping under him. Eric opened his mouth and screamed into the oncoming wall of air. He could scarcely hear himself, yet he yelled hard enough to make his throat feel scratchy.

A bolt. A thunderclap.

One second; the lightning had cracked within a quarter mile of the house.

Everything around Eric was now in terrific motion, a whirring blur of leaf and branch, but he clung to the tree and screamed again and again into the teeth of the storm, wild from the excitement of it.

And then there was another flash, this one blinding him, crashing into his ear like the explosion of a cannon, so that for a terrifying instant he thought he had been struck. His head rang from the reverberation, his hands trembled against the tree, and the downpour lashed him furiously like countless fire hoses gone mad.

Another flash, another roll of thunder. But these occurred beyond the garden, already moving across the ravine toward the distant row of backyards. He strained to see what could not be seen—the brutish musculature of the unseen wind striking down bush and branch. Sheets of rain still battered at the garden after the major thrust of the storm winds moved on. Eric wiped the rain from his eyes and squinted through the thick gray light at the lawn, feeling beneath his body the living surge of the oak tree, as it was shaken from leaf to root by another shudder of wind.

An idea took hold of him: If the tree survived, so would he; if the tree toppled, so would he. They would live or die together! Again he bellowed defiantly into the tremendous air, watching twigs and leaves, borne on the boiling wind, swirl through the rain. The breakneck beauty of the storm so awed him that when finally it began subsiding, Eric wished for it to last longer, to last forever.

Then, breathless, he watched the final thunderheads

sweep lumpishly by, trailing in their heavy wake the most delicate filaments of cloud, as if some white cotton had pulled free. The light changed radically, assuming colors of varying gray that his sight hardly registered before becoming other grays; the changing light made it seem for a few moments as if time had been speeded up, as if the earth itself were spinning faster.

Then a rainbow twinkled on the lawn, shimmered there for a few tremulous moments that reminded him of what he had read in a weather book: a rainbow is the ghost of a butterfly. It was. It was!

And the sun slanted hotly upon the grass which began to recover its uprightness. Eric looked at the world coming back to itself: the dripping leaves, the glistening bark, the branches easing into their old positions. He slid down the trunk, feeling his shoes squish, and trudged out into the middle of the lawn. Wavering lines of moisture were already snaking up into the sky to make yet other clouds and new storms. Things gleamed. He flung himself into the grass, smelling the rich scent of the freshened earth. Near his eye was a bead of water pulling loose slowly from a blade of grass. He strained to watch until the two objects seemed enormous, like a round planet pulling free from the side of the universe, two things of elemental force in the farthest reaches of space.

And then the drop of water fell, losing its roundness on a tiny shard of gravel. Eric turned over and gazed at the sky. Never had he enjoyed the garden so much. Never had he felt closer to it.

Something caught his eye.

Eric sat upright and stared in amazement at the hickory

tree. One of the sturdy middle limbs had been sheared away from the trunk, as if brutally axed through. The branches of the shorn limb pointed earthward, held suspended by the weight of other branches. The ragged wound in the hickory trunk looked to Eric like the gap left by a pulled tooth—raw, ugly. And then he realized that the lightning had done it. The bolt that had temporarily blinded and deafened him had struck but twenty feet away. It might as easily have struck the oak—and him.

That possibility increased his keen enjoyment of the storm's aftermath. It had been a serious confrontation, not just a game. He might have died in that storm. Never again would he try his luck by riding out a storm from a tree, but this once he had tried it and been lucky. The oak, the hickory, the whole garden, had conspired to protect him from danger. Eric glanced slowly around in wonder. He didn't believe in magic, yet here it was, surrounding him. The garden was sacred.

Eric stretched out with a sigh and flung his arms back into the wet grass, luxuriating in the sensation of feeling the hot dry sun on his face and the wet cool grass against his back. In his mind he went first into the dry hot world, then into the wet cool one, sliding effortlessly from the consciousness of one sensation to the other.

He must have fallen into a deep sleep then, because from a long way off he heard Mister Beck calling and calling. Eric opened his eyes wide and met the immaculate blue of a sky swept clear of clouds.

"Eric? Eric?" The old man's voice rose in alarm. "Are you okay? Eric?"

He raised up on one elbow and turned to see the old man

fighting through the screen door with one hand, while poking the cane out with the other.

Eric rushed to help him.

"Saw you from the kitchen," Mister Beck panted. "Lying on the ground. I thought for a moment—there was a crash. . . ."

"Lightning hit there." Eric pointed at the hickory tree and took the old man's arm.

"Then I was right. You could have been hurt," observed Mister Beck anxiously.

"Don't worry. I was safe," Eric lied.

He felt sudden guilt for having forgotten all about the old man during the storm. It had never once crossed his mind, while in the tree, that Mister Beck had been sitting helpless and small in a dark room. While lightning and thunder swept across the roof, the old man had been hunched in the corner of a sofa, worrying about him. But if he said anything or apologized, Mr. Beck would laugh it off. Mister Beck would say, "If you concentrated on the storm, you didn't have time for anything else. Did you or did you not go out to concentrate on the storm? Well, then!"

As if the old man had read his mind, Mister Beck said, "How did the storm go?"

Eric helped him lower his unsteady body into the chair.

"I'll never forget it." Then Eric added, "I forgot about you."

"Forgot about me? Well, what of it?"

Eric shrugged.

"What is it? You want to take me along?" Mister Beck's voice was tough, cold, accusing. "Don't you know you can't do that? When you look at something, you look at it. You can't take people along, Eric. Just as I can't take you along into those paintings of mine you don't like."

Eric opened his mouth to deny that he disliked them, but the old man silenced him by raising a trembling but peremptory hand.

"You don't like my paintings," Mister Beck declared, "and why should you? They are the result of my looking at something. I put in plenty of time looking at that prison, so the result is mine. Now this garden is yours. I'm only giving you a method and the opportunity and nothing more. Don't include me. What you see is yours."

Then Mister Beck closed his eyes. "If you are going to sit, sit. I have two of those damn pills in me, and they tell me to sleep."

So Eric entered a new square that afternoon, letting one hour among zinnias and marigolds stretch almost into two.

And the days followed, one square after another, with the summer filling with heat and green smells, with stone flies and bees, with grasshoppers and butterflies. The garden hummed. Eric sat. Mister Beck dozed. And one by one each square was confronted, lived in, left.

The Town ✿

He had to put in an appearance at Larry's. He should have
gone there a week ago, but somehow he had kept putting
it off until the situation looked serious. If Roddy could
follow him to the garden and spy, so could the gang. The
longer he avoided them, the more curious they'd become.

And he wanted to see them. They were his friends, even
though he sometimes felt uneasy around them. The fact
was, they stood behind him; they shared his indifference to
school, his contempt for joining organizations. They were
all held together by their difference from other kids who,
like Silky, for example, played the game according to adult
rules.

So that afternoon when he entered Larry's, he was disappointed when he didn't see the gang.

Then he noticed Bones sitting at the far end of the
counter. A baseball cap was perched on top of the thick
black hair.

Eric joined him but without more than a glance. It wasn't

pleasant looking at Bones, who had a faceful of pimples and waxy ears.

"Where have *you* been?" Bones asked in a voice of accusation that he had picked up from Horse, who was always accusing people of things.

This was a question Eric had anticipated. He claimed to have been doing a lot of yard work at home.

Bones nodded without conviction. It was clear to Eric that the gang had given his whereabouts plenty of thought. They had probably biked around the house just to see for themselves if he had been working in the yard. But it was too late now; Eric had offered an excuse and would have to stick with it.

"How's probation going?" Bones asked after ordering another Coke.

"Can't complain."

"Sergeant Nolan won't be interviewing us next week. He's going on vacation. He keeps asking me if we have been hanging out together."

"He asks me, too."

"This last time," Bones continued, "he asked did I see you, and naturally I said no, and he asked then was I hanging out with the old man who got out of prison—that killer. I said, What killer? But he wouldn't tell me. He said, if you don't know, it won't hurt you." Bones ran long fingers through his shaggy hair. Eric glanced sidelong at him just in time to see Bones do something that was especially unpleasant. Bones stuck a finger in his ear and turned it like a cork in a bottle. Eric looked away quickly, not wanting to see him draw it out.

"Cops have got to be kind of stupid," Bones went on.

"Like the sergeant asks me about this killer who got out of prison and when I ask who, won't tell me the guy's name."

So Nolan was asking other kids if they knew Mister Beck. That meant Nolan hadn't forgotten about it.

"But I found out," said Bones.

"Found out what?"

"Who this killer who got out is. An old guy living over on Norris Street."

"How do you know?" Eric asked, trying not to sound too curious.

"Everybody knows. That's why Nolan is so stupid. Won't tell me who he's asking me do I hang out with, but you can't keep a killer secret. Right? Not in this town where I bet the last murder committed here was before we were even born."

"Two years ago," Eric said, "that guy robbed Philips' Drug Store, and Mr. Philips shot him dead."

"That wasn't murder, that was self-defense," Bones argued. "Anyway—"

Eric had to admit that Bones was right; Mister Beck's presence was becoming common knowledge. Then Eric thought of a question, a kind of probe to test the situation. "Who did this old man kill?"

"I don't know that," Bones said. "But he lives with his daughter here in town. I heard my mother talking about it on the phone. His daughter's the one has that gift shop on —" Bones scratched his head, pushing the baseball cap forward on his pimply brow. "I forget the street. But she has this gift shop."

"I got to get to work," Eric said and paid for his Coke. "Tell the guys I came by."

"When are you going to honor us with your presence again?" It was a sarcastic phrase that Bones had picked up from Zap, who used it often.

"Tomorrow," Eric replied immediately.

And he did. The next day he showed his face at Larry's and went with the gang to the bowling alley. The guys accepted him back into their midst, but something was different; there was a kind of caution in their treatment of him, as if he were on probation again. But he had a hard time thinking about the gang because Mister Beck occupied most of his thoughts. Never had Eric felt so helpless in his life, knowing that he could not stem the tide of gossip in this town. Within a week there would probably not be a living soul in Forest Park above five years old who did not know of the paroled murderer living on Norris Street.

During the succeeding days at Larry's or the bowling alley or the pool or at home, Eric overheard people discussing the Becks. Even the gang mentioned them with a kind of grudging respect, as if Mr. Beck and his daughter were celebrities. Everywhere Eric went he heard snatches of conversation about them. The town seemed to polarize over the issue of the Becks. Some people believed in the principle of live and let live; if the old man had paid his debt with forty years of imprisonment, that should be enough. Others railed at the authorities for paroling such a hardened criminal. Still others took the position that the law-abiding citizenry of the town must be protected. Horse's parents, for example, believed that the Becks should be forced to leave Forest Park.

This was ominous talk indeed, based as it was on the fact that a very old man had spent forty years of his life in prison for unspecified murder. What would the reaction be, Eric asked himself gloomily, when people learned that Mister Beck had murdered his own wife?

While this dismaying question remained unanswered, the town interest in the Becks took a more serious turn. Standing in the hallway near the veranda, Eric heard his parents talking one night over cocktails; Mother was describing a meeting that day of The Concerned Citizens League at which it was suggested that The Lonely Hunter ought to be boycotted. "The woman has run that gift shop here for at least fifteen years," Mother continued hotly. "I think it's downright disgusting to punish her for something her father did. Sometimes I despise people."

Eric felt a rush of gratitude for his mother's stand.

But then events began to accelerate. Only a few days later, when he was having his hair cut, a customer in the next chair began to describe the latest development. He was a large florid man with his chin fully lathered. He said to the barber, "Hear the latest about those Becks? People are boycotting the daughter's store."

"You don't say," murmured the barber. "I heard some were buying from her out of sympathy."

"Out of foolish ignorance," snorted the customer. "Wait till they know the whole story of this Beck fella."

Then came the dreaded words that Eric knew would come, that he hoped would not come, that ultimately he and the Becks must deal with.

"He killed his wife."

"You don't say." The barber whistled lowly and slid the long razor with a single stroke along the customer's ruddy jawline.

"Who's going to buy from a woman," continued the

customer, "who brings home the man who killed her own mother?"

"I see the point," said the barber, maneuvering around the red face.

"I wouldn't be surprised," added the customer, "if the landlord doesn't use a clause in the lease to throw her out before she even has time to go broke. What's the world coming to? Now you can murder your wife, and your children give you a place to stay."

The barber clicked his tongue.

It was all that Eric could do to keep seated until his hair had been cut. Once outside, he climbed on his bike and pedaled aimlessly for a long time down the hot drowsy streets. Why did people have to interfere in the life of an old dying man? It wasn't fair. Mother was right about that. And yet sooner or later—sooner—she and Father would hear the whole truth about the Becks and insist that he stop seeing the old man. If not tonight, then tomorrow. He figured that from their point of view they had already stretched tolerance to the limit. How could he argue against them? And yet whatever they told him, however they tried to get a promise out of him, he would not desert Mister Beck. Each day in the garden with Mister Beck strengthened the bond between them. He imagined them alone in the garden; it was a fantasy in the hot afternoon: squad-car lights were turning in the driveway, while helmeted cops, led by Sergeant Nolan, called at them with megaphones to come out of the garden, but before he could help Mister Beck take a single step from the chair, the garden seemed to be surrounded by thick fog, and suddenly he and Mister Beck realized that the world beyond the garden had been rendered invisible—or the garden to the rest of the world —and they were floating outside of time.

The sweat poured from Eric's face. Pumping his bike into high speed, he set course for the Beck house.

❀ ❀ ❀

The garden shimmered from the wings of insects catching the noonday light. But Eric didn't notice. He ran across the lawn toward the huddled figure in the chair, crying out, "Mister Beck! It's wrong! It's wrong!"

Startled, the old man twisted around and stared from sleep-dulled eyes at the boy.

"They shouldn't do that to her," Eric said breathlessly, flinging himself down beside the chair.

"Do what to whom?" Mister Beck asked, arranging the shawl around his neck.

"To your—daughter." It sounded strange in Eric's ear to call a woman of Miss Beck's age a daughter. A daughter to him meant someone closer to his own age.

"You mean what's happening in this town? Is that it?"

"Some people are really stupid," Eric mumbled.

"Oh, it's not so much stupidity as it is fear of the unknown," commented Mister Beck. Then, in a new musing voice, he added, "The poor woman, though. She never had much in life, and now this. Stayed loyal to me all these years. Isn't that amazing?"

They were silent a while. Then Mister Beck said in a thoughtful voice, as if explaining something to himself as well as to Eric, "I told her when they paroled me that I could do all right in a home. She could come and visit me there, but my girl, my Sophia, wouldn't have it. She said she

had worked hard to buy this house for the both of us. Can
you imagine that? It was a gamble, her bringing me here,
and she lost it." There was a choked sob from the old man.

Eric looked quickly away and saw the squirrel Roger
leaping through the pin oak, thrusting its sharp arrogant
face between some leaves to regard angrily a wren that had
perched momentarily on a twig. Roger was like people, Eric
thought; guarding what he thinks is his even when it isn't.

"Oh, well," said Mister Beck with a sigh, "Sophia and I
can make a go of it."

Eric squinted at him and asked tremulously, "Then you
won't leave town?"

"No, we won't leave town," Mister Beck said with a faint
smile. "There are savings. Hers. Sophia isn't the sort of
woman you can push around. No one is going to throw her
out of her own house." Mister Beck chuckled. "And the art
dealer is coming down from Chicago to look at my paintings. Who knows? He might make me rich."

Eric had no faith in that way of getting money. But he was
immensely relieved to know that the Becks would not leave
town, that each day the old man would be sitting in this
garden.

"I'm surprised at you, Eric," Mister Beck said with a
sudden frown. "You haven't mentioned something very
important."

Eric looked at him quizzically.

"Only two squares left to go, and you haven't even mentioned the possibility of finishing the whole garden today."

He had known that he would finish today, but what about
tomorrow?

※ ※ ※

Having finished the last square, Eric trudged gloomily to his bike leaning against the garage. He had a flat tire, so decided to leave it until tomorrow. He felt overcome by fatigue for no real reason. He felt sad, depressed, as if something had been lost. Passing the old man who dozed in the chair, Eric left the garden by the ravine. No sooner had he reached the bottom and set out through the undergrowth than he heard someone yelling. A woman stood at the top of the ravine, about a half-dozen houses north of the Becks'. She was gesturing vigorously down at Eric.

He pointed to his chest. "Me?"

"Come here a minute! Please!"

He climbed the steep gully and found himself alongside a squat gray-haired woman in a house smock. Her hands, clasped in front of her, seemed to be pleading.

"I thought it was you," the woman said breathlessly and stared at him from gray eyes enlarged by thick glasses. "I thought I saw you down there. I told myself, just find out. And it was!" She kept her hands clasped as if in supplication. "Would you take a Coke? I have them. I won't keep you long. It was just I had to speak to you someday, and this seemed it."

Eric glanced at a chair placed at the edge of the ravine. The woman must sit in it and sun herself during the day; she had a tanned parched face. The yard was indifferently kept, the grass long and weedy, the single flower bed sparsely planted with peonies and zinnias ragged from the despoliation of insects. Fastened to a clothesline running widthwise across the lawn was a rope leading down to the collar of an extremely fat bulldog who eyed Eric suspiciously. Its huge red tongue lolled over one side of a cavernous mouth. Its muzzle was white with age.

"That's Alfred," explained the woman. "He's protection. Know what I mean? What's your name, dear?"

Eric stared at the clasped hands, the thick glasses, the parted lips above which ran a faint line of blonde mustache. "Eric," he told her.

"Eric what? I have a whole six pack of Cokes. How about one? What did you say—Eric what?"

"Fischer. No, thank you."

"I want you to meet Alfred."

Eric allowed her to lead him forward with her beckoning clasped hands toward the thing looking more like a huge toad than a dog. When they had come almost into range, Alfred struggled to his feet—the back ones unfolding like pieces of pressed rubber, slowly, stiffly—and panted harder.

"Don't go closer," the woman advised Eric suddenly. "He's perfectly harmless—aren't you, you poor sad thing? Only if he doesn't know people, he tries to protect me." She leaned down, and Alfred, grunting, flicked out his broad tongue and heavily swiped her face with it, leaving a trail of slime. The woman did not wipe it off, but straightened up and grinned triumphantly at Eric. "Alfred is so sweet because I give him all the love I possess. What was the name again?"

"Eric Fischer."

"I can never remember names. I can't remember faces either," the woman admitted, leading the way back to her chair. "People look like mice to me. Isn't that funny? Where do you live, Eric Fischer?"

He told her.

Her face brightened with respect. "Oh, I know that neighborhood. It's very classy. I knew someone who lived over that way. It was—it was—" Her soft broad face went blank. "Someone. I forget. Sure about that Coke? I have six of them cold in the refrigerator."

Eric saw gold flash in her mouth. Her hands, still clasped, seemed to be eternally in prayer. She seemed pretty nuts to him. He didn't trust that old dog, either, no matter how fat it was, and the more Eric regarded the woman, the more her soft broad face resembled that of Alfred.

"I better be going," Eric said.

"Wait! Wait a minute!" the woman cried and touched his arm. It was the first time her hands had unclasped. Leaning forward, she glanced around as if they could be easily overheard in a crowded room. "I got this question to ask, Eric Fischer." She put one finger coyly to her lips. "Mum's the word. Just between us, tell me what he's really like."

Eric took a backward step away from her. "I have to go home."

The woman advanced, her eyes widening behind the thick lenses. "I know you go over there every day and sit in his yard. Everybody knows about it," she said frowning. "I just want to know what he's really like."

"I have to go home," Eric muttered. "The family's expecting—"

"Murders, for example. Does he talk about how he did them? Does he feel sorry? Or is he cold-blooded? He looks it to me; only you can't tell a book by its cover." She advanced as fast as Eric was retreating. "Don't worry about my saying anything to anybody. I keep my mouth shut in this neighborhood. People around here have a common streak a mile wide." She grabbed for Eric, but he had reached the edge of her yard and started down the ravine.

"Wait a minute!" she called after him. "Come back here! Who do you think you are?"

He went fast down the ravine, not glancing behind him, not even when her voice filled the ravine with its shrieking: "Nasty boy! Nasty boy! Shame on your folks! Shame! Nasty boy!"

Shaken by the encounter, Eric plowed through the gully brambles in a kind of panic. Until now he had never thought much about the Becks' neighbors. He and Mister Beck had never left the garden, and while they were inside it, no one else really existed for them beyond it. But now as he made his way through the ravine, he glanced up at the row of yards visible from the bottom pathway, as if he were a soldier on patrol, wary of ambush.

※ ※ ※

Eric braced himself for a confrontation at home—and it came. This time his parents called him formally into the study instead of trapping him in the family room. They did not criticize him at all; in fact, Mother spent a long time expressing her contempt for a lot of people in town who lacked the imagination to conceive of that old man as being more than an evil beast. After all, it had been a *crime passionnel*—Mother had obviously gone back into newspaper files and researched the case—not a cold-blooded premeditated murder, which is why the court had let him off with a life sentence instead of the chair. But do people listen? No. They exercise themselves over ways to hurt a dying man and a daughter brave enough and generous enough to give him a few days of peace after forty years of penance. Mother could be eloquent in her anger. Father sat nodding in his agreement and puffing on his pipe for emphasis.

But at last his parents turned directly to Eric. The righteous indignation against busybodies had been a kind of prologue to the real point: the necessity for him to quit seeing Mister Beck. Father led the argument by sensibly laying out the danger. People inflamed by the spirit of retribution often do impulsive things. They might camp on the Beck doorstep or burn a cross on the lawn or commit acts of vandalism. If Eric were present, he might become— Father emphasized the word—*physically* involved. And it all could lead to the police, and that, of course, would bring Sergeant Nolan into the affair and the whole matter of probation. Father put it all logically and calmly, which was the reason for his being a successful businessman.

At last, when Father fell silent and his parents both regarded him anxiously, Eric drew a deep breath and said, "He needs me even more now."

Father puffed vigorously on his pipe.

"We don't want you getting hurt," said Mother.

"We don't want you in more trouble with the police," added Father.

"I'm the only friend he's got," declared Eric without raising his voice. "I won't desert him." Plainly his parents did not know what to do. It suddenly occurred to Eric that he was making them suffer; it wasn't just a matter of him against them. But he could not back down. Never. "I won't," he added in such a resolute tone of voice that he seemed to snap his parents' resistance. It was as if he had decided the question for them—almost to their relief. Because after a few sighs and coughs they let him leave the study with a single promise, with hardly another word.

But upstairs he ran into opposition of a more vehement nature.

Susan, appearing in her doorway, crooked her finger at him. "Come in here," she ordered him briskly.

Eric stepped into the room that otherwise was strictly off limits. He looked at the college pennants on the wall, the heap of clothes in a chair, the phonograph records removed from their sleeves and scattered across the bed. Gingerly he sat on the edge of it.

Susan was pacing in jeans and a hastily buttoned shirt; she must have heard him on the stairs and thrown something on to intercept him before he got to his own room. "I can't figure you out," she began. "What can you find to do with a man that old? Roddy says you sit in his garden playing some kind of game. What in hell kind of game is it?"

"He's teaching me to look at the garden."

Susan's eyes widened with surprise and anger. "What? Look at the *what?*" She threw her hands up in a gesture of frustration probably learned as a member of the school drama club. "How do you think I feel?" she continued and leaned toward him.

Eric could see her bra through the half-buttoned shirt. He stared until Susan, aware of him doing it, straightened up and did the buttons quickly. "I asked you a question," she mumbled bitterly.

"What was it?"

"You know, Eric, you are really and truly exasperating. First you land on probation; then you get drunk at the pool in front of Danny Richmond, and now you take up with an old murderer. How would *you* like to have a brother like that?" Susan was pacing dramatically. "Of course I wouldn't expect you to give a damn. Your friends are a bunch of misfits, so naturally you don't suffer from your actions." She turned in front of the Yale pennant. "But I do; I suffer. Because I have worthwhile friends. And Mother and Father, they suffer plenty. Did it ever occur to you that they have a reputation to think of in this town? You have really hurt them, Eric. Which is why I never told them about that incident at the pool. I figured it would only hurt them more, and since they couldn't do anything about it, why add to their misery?"

She halted this time in front of Illinois. Susan had worked herself into a passion of righteous indignation. And yet even though she was acting dramatically, Eric knew that she meant what she said. Otherwise she would have told on him. It had surprised him for a long time that she had kept her promise not to tell. One thing about Susan: she loved their parents. It was her best trait, in his opinion.

"Well?" she said, hands on hips. "Doesn't it bother you one bit that you're hurting them?"

Eric got up, glancing at Georgia Tech, Columbia, Northwestern, and UCLA arranged in a pinwheel pattern. At the door he turned and met Susan's blue-shadowed eyes until hers broke contact. "Sure it bothers me," he said. "Only the old man is my friend. Nothing you can say will ever change that."

"You'll be sorry!" Susan called after him.

He already was. He was sorry for causing his parents so much trouble. He hadn't given them much thought when he was put on probation, but now he did. He now had a glimpse of a town's power, of its collective spite, and he understood that his parents wanted to protect him from such reality. They must feel terribly frustrated because he was preventing them from giving him help. Susan was wrong; it bothered him a lot. And he was sorry for hurting them.

But he was not sorry for holding fast to his decision.

※ ※ ※

He was going through the ravine and then thought better of it. He didn't want them up there staring down at him. So he climbed out of the gully and walked the last quarter of mile along the street, glaring defiantly at each house, many having the blinds drawn against the morning sunshine. He wished for someone to come out on a porch and say something. He'd halt and stare—just that—just stare until the person couldn't return his stare. Then he would laugh and walked off without looking back. That's what he hoped for, but nothing happened. Maybe they were all peeking at him from behind the curtains, the bunch of cowards.

Then he saw the Beck house, a service truck of some kind parked in front of it. Approaching, Eric noticed a man inserting a pane of glass in a front window. There was broken glass on the lawn and walk. Miss Beck was on her hands and knees, scooping it into a trash bag. Three other windows were also broken, and for a dismaying moment Eric recalled the rocks he had thrown at the school. He understood at last the nature of that sort of violence; it was like those people sneaking looks at him from their closed houses; it was cowardly, violent and cowardly. He would never throw rocks again.

Eric knelt beside the woman and started picking up glass, too.

Their eyes met briefly. Then they worked in silence until the glass was in the trash bag.

"Thank you, Eric," said Miss Beck with the trace of a smile.

He nodded solemnly and went around the side of the house. Mister Beck waved gaily from his chair as if nothing had happened.

"Guess what? That art dealer from Chicago called this morning. He's coming to see my paintings."

Eric had turned slightly to hear the service truck drive away.

"Ah, don't worry about that," Mister Beck said disdainfully. "Some punks did it. Drove by in a car and tossed a few rocks."

Eric wondered if it could have been anyone he knew. Like any of the high school crowd in Susan's class. Or that barber-shop customer and some cronies. He would have suspected the gang, but they didn't have a car. Six months ago, maybe, he would have gone along with them if they had said, "Hey, let's go get that old jailbird." Eric shook his head at the wonder of it.

"It's none of my business," began Mister Beck, shading his eyes from the glare to get a good look at Eric, "but you never mention your family."

It was the first time the family had ever been mentioned. "There's nothing to say," he replied.

"Oh, I'm not prying. They are none of my business. But

I can't help wondering if they know you come here."

"They know."

"And they let you come?"

Eric hesitated, then decided to tell the truth. "They're against it."

Mister Beck nodded and said, "I would imagine so. With you on probation, they are afraid of your friendship with an ex-con. I think you'd better give up coming here for a while, Eric."

"No, sir."

"I said for a while."

"No, sir."

"Come on, Eric, be sensible. Until this thing blows over."

"No, sir." Eric added, "This is our summer. We can't wait."

Mister Beck regarded him for a moment, then smiled. "I can't argue with that logic. I just want you to understand the possible danger of your coming into this garden."

"I have to come here."

"You still feel that way, after finishing the squares?"

"Even more now."

"Why?"

"Because I did all that sitting and don't know why I did it. So I have to find out."

Mister Beck pursed his lips thoughtfully. "Yes, I suppose you do. My method only got you started. Now you're on your own, because you haven't really finished with the garden. But didn't you think it would be all over with the last square?"

"Yes, I guess I did."

"And now you know it hasn't ended at all."

Eric squinted through the blinding light at the old face; it was like looking at an old tree, something weathered by the seasons, dry and solid, something with roots deep inside the earth. "I guess I'll just hang around the garden," Eric said finally, "and see what happens."

Mister Beck slapped the arm of his chair for emphasis. "Good! In your place it's what I'd do. It's a way to begin."

"I think," said Eric, "I'll go up there a while." He strolled over to the pin oak and proceeded to climb it.

Midway up the tree Eric felt a cool breeze; the sound of it swishing past his ears drowned out the sounds of the neighborhood. He glanced across the rooftops, acutely aware of people inside some of those houses not wanting him to be here any more than they wanted Mister Beck to be sitting on the lawn beneath him. But that was all right. He didn't know why, but he felt nothing could harm Mister Beck and himself when they were inside the garden. Maybe the lightning bolt that had come within twenty feet of killing him had convinced him of the magical protectiveness of the garden. And there in the pin oak he felt that everything was trustworthy and comforting below him. A kind of invisible but indestructible balloon of air hovered around the Beck garden, protecting the three of them, because he included Miss Beck, too.

Across the rooftops a squadron of ducks was flying. Each autumn thousands of birds flew in mass formation above the town, navigating southward by the position of the sun.

Summer was moving on.

Eric glanced down and to his relief saw Mister Beck holding a glass of lemonade. The old man was all right, because the garden would look after all three of them. The garden was sacred.

※   ※   ※

The next day Eric met the gang at the bowling alley. He never had been much of a bowler, although he could match Zap in a contest. Superkool never lost to anyone except a couple of the big-shot bowlers who bowled in the local league.

Today the gang had an alley next to that being used by a bunch of girls from school who were giggling and glancing sidelong at Horse. Horse wasn't older than the rest of the gang, but he looked older because of his height and the breadth of his shoulders. The girls never gave Solo a second look, although in the last year he had grown taller than most of the girls in his class. Today, however, that wasn't exactly the truth; one rather timid girl, Sally Wilson, had given him a long thoughtful stare, making him feel uncomfortably as if they were alone together in an empty room. He stopped looking at the girls after that, although every time he grasped the bowling ball and went into his approach for releasing it, he had this feeling of being watched and so he threw with more power than accuracy, causing the ball to spin furiously into the pins with a crack more dramatic than effective.

The gang seemed to be outdoing themselves, too, because of the girls. There was more roughhouse and loud talking than usual. Then after Solo took his turn and threw a lucky, vicious strike, causing him to glance quickly at the girls, he felt upon his return to the table a hard blow in his ribs. He turned to face Zap.

"What was that for?" Zap had hit him far harder than normal roughhousing warranted.

Zap's roving eye slid in its gaze past Solo's shoulder. "For nothing," Zap said with a sneer. "It's free of charge."

Horse, having thrown his ball down the alley, turned and laughed. "Ah, leave him alone, Zap. The poor kid's in love."

Zap giggled. Superkool giggled and got up for his turn. "No kidding," said Zap. "Who's he in love with?"

"Didn't you hear about the old jailbird?" replied Horse. "Solo and him have got this thing about birds and bees, flowers and trees."

So they knew. Eric was not at all surprised. He had been waiting for days for them to say something. Perhaps they had waited for the proper time, say, when they were bowling next to a bunch of girls. He glanced at the next alley. A couple of the girls were listening. Sally Wilson was listening.

"Come on," Zap said, giving him another fierce poke in the ribs. "What do you and the old jailbird do? Plan murders?"

Solo held both arms against his ribs. "Don't poke me like that."

"What do you and him do?" Zap persisted, rising for his turn.

"Yeah," said Superkool, sitting down. "Does he talk about crime and stuff? Does he tell you how to blow a guy away?"

"Let him alone," said Solo, glancing at the next alley. She was listening.

"Let him alone?" Superkool was on his feet, grimacing

in every direction. "Where is he? How can we let him alone if we don't know where he is?"

The guys giggled. Eric heard giggling from the next alley. He looked that way; she was not even smiling, but her eyes were fixed on him.

Now it was his turn to bowl, but before he could pick up the ball, Horse had beat him to it. Holding Eric's bowling ball in one big hand high in the air, he thundered, "Eric Fischer! We want to meet your friend!"

The other guys took up the chant. "Eric Fischer! We want to meet your friend!"

One of the girls leaned over the railing and whispered something to Superkool, who whispered something back. The girl tittered and reported to her friends.

Solo wasn't sure what to do. It was clear that the gang had not forgiven him for deserting their company. It was also clear that they envied him his relationship with a notorious killer. He glanced at the other alley where all four girls were regarding him curiously. All were smiling, too, except her, Sally Wilson, who continued to stare at him as if they were alone together in an empty room.

Then Horse lowered the bowling ball and let it fall into Solo's outstretched hands.

Solo took his turn. A gutter ball. There was laughter behind him, so before turning and facing it, he closed his eyes a moment, seeing the garden in which everything was moving through the sunshine like the sea.

One of the girls was leaning over the rail again, her eyes on Solo, her ear close to Superkool's lips.

"What's going on?" Solo could not help but ask.

Superkool straightened up and thrust his hands in his

pockets. In a loud voice he said, "I was just answering a question about you and the jailbird. She wants to know what you do. I told her the old man sits in a chair and you sit in the grass. You don't do anything. You sit and the old guy sleeps. I've seen you. It's really fantastic." Superkool grinned maliciously.

Solo felt himself being spun around by a powerful grip. He looked up into Horse's broad face.

"We want to meet him," Horse declared. "Here you've been learning all about the guy and never told us a damn thing. Why hold out, huh? We want to meet this guy and see what he has to say."

"Yeah," said Superkool, sauntering up and pulling his knife from a back pocket. He flipped all three blades out. "I bet the old jailbird doesn't know these are ACA blades." He flashed the knife close enough to make Eric jerk back. "That means amazing cutting action," he said and swiped the air again, causing the girls nearby to cry out in fear and excitement. Superkool turned and bowed deeply to them. "Don't worry, girls," he said. "See this?" He held the knife by the sheepfoot blade and shoved the handle forward, displaying an antiqued brass crest. "This is the American eagle. This is a patriotic knife."

The girls giggled merrily, all except Sally Wilson who was watching Solo back away.

"Hey, where are you going, Eric Fischer?" yelled Horse.

So it really was Eric Fischer. Gone was Solo. Good, Eric thought, as he pushed past Zap and left the alley.

"We want to meet that guy!" called Superkool, waving his knife through the air.

"We want to help run him out of town!" added Horse.

"Go on, get back to your old jailbird!" crowed Zap and laughed.

Eric glanced back once, but not at the gang—at Sally Wilson, whose eyes met his in that strange uncomfortable way. As for the gang, Eric thought, when he got to his bike, he wanted nothing to do with them anymore. He didn't mind them pushing him around a little; that was what some guys did. But he hated their jealousy. He hated them for begrudging him some time with another friend. Who were they to tell him what to do? They'd never let him back in the gang, but more importantly, he wouldn't even try.

⚡ ⚡ ⚡

For the next few days Eric watched for signs of trouble around the Beck house. Cars cruised up and down Norris Street, slowing in front of the clapboard house so that whole families could gawk at the residence of a maniacal killer. From the open window Eric heard the phone ringing constantly. Miss Beck never answered it, although she was home all the time now. Mister Beck claimed that the gift shop was closed for inventory, but Eric knew better. It was closed because of the boycott. People were trying to squeeze the Becks out of town either by ruining her business or by threatening them with violence. He figured there must be plenty of unsigned mail coming to the house, just as there had been in a television drama he had once seen.

One afternoon, when he was reading in the grass, Eric had the strange feeling that he was being watched. Glancing up, he met the curious stare of a middle-aged couple standing in the driveway next to the Beck garage. The woman pulled the man's sleeve and whispered something, shielding her mouth with the other hand as if afraid of being overheard. They made no attempt to leave, but stood there, watching him watch them.

Then Miss Beck burst out of the house, seemingly propelled out of the mouth of a cannon, her mouth filled with shouted words even before she had got past the screen door.

"You two! You in the driveway! What do you want here?" she yelled querulously. "What is it? Tell me!"

Eric was startled by the power of her voice. It had the same resonance that Mister Beck's voice had when he wanted to use it. Until this moment Eric had only heard the woman speak in a calm low tone, as if she were prepared to accommodate herself to any situation, no matter how disagreeable. But now she was another woman. She wasn't going to let that prying couple get away easily. She'd shame them with her voice that had become a powerful instrument of vengeance. "What do you want here!" She was on their heels, yelling in a thunderous voice. "I demand you tell me! What have you been doing in my driveway? What you are sneaking around for? What do you want?"

Eric watched the couple, with Miss Beck right behind them, disappear around the side of the house. Long after the three were gone, he heard her voice, scaring those two people to death, shaming them in front of a whole neighborhood.

At last Miss Beck returned, and Eric got to his feet and gave her a cheer, "Hooray!" as if she had just run for a touchdown.

Miss Beck hardly gave him a glance, but head lowered,

she strode rapidly into the house and banged the screen
door shut.

Mister Beck was chuckling.

Eric looked at him. The curious thing about Mister Beck
was, none of this really bothered him. Not deeply. As long
as his daughter could handle the situation without too much
grief, the old man was satisfied. Of course, it was possible
that Mister Beck was riding high on the slim chance of
selling those paintings. The art dealer from Chicago had
come to look at the work and had complimented Mister
Beck and given him to understand that more than compli-
ments were in the offing, although Eric felt it was wrong to
get up an old man's hopes like that. And yet even the
outside hope of selling his paintings was not enough to
account for Mister Beck's serenity in the face of such inva-
sion. Windows had been broken and garbage dumped on
the front walk and someone had painted GET OUT in red
letters across the steps, but Mister Beck only shrugged. He
wasn't touched by such things. Maybe he had suffered too
much ever to worry about the opinion of people in this
town. To watch him sit and let people stare at him like an
animal in the zoo and never complain, never even get angry
or frustrated, was a lesson that Eric meant to take to heart.
He would treat these foolish assaults on the garden the way
Mister Beck did.

Let people do what they wished; there was still the garden, always the garden. Even if this whole neighborhood
and every neighborhood in town descended on the Beck
place, breaking and destroying everything, trampling the
flowers and knocking over the birdbath, uprooting trees,
wrecking the hedges, grinding ant and grasshopper under-

foot, and generally ruining the entire garden, it wouldn't matter. It wouldn't really matter, because the garden would somehow still be his and Mister Beck's and Miss Beck's, too. Nothing could take the garden away from them, because it was not so much the layout of it or the things planted in it as it was the earth beneath it and the sky above it that mattered, and the insects and birds and wildlife, like Roger playing watchman in the pin-oak tree and the rabbits hopping through at dawn and the blue racer slithering through the grass. He and the Becks would return to the garden even if people ravaged it so it did not look recognizable, because the animals knew where the garden really was; it was in themselves and the Becks. It was in himself, too. All this time he had been looking for something in the garden, when really what he had been looking for had been inside of himself. He had been sitting inside of himself in each square and hadn't known it. The garden was everywhere. It flowed from one thing to another like water that was lapping endlessly out of a secret well. There was no getting hold of it; there was no letting go of it, either. It couldn't be lost once it was found. It was forever.

Eric was suddenly aware of tears rolling down his cheeks. He glanced quickly at the chair, but Mister Beck had fallen asleep.

Out loud, even though he knew the old man did not hear him, Eric said, "We're going to be all right. Nothing can happen to us." Eric said calmly, "We have this garden."

The Attack 🌿

The next morning Eric awoke and looked at a sky without color. Roddy was already up and gone. Probably the whole family was gone, because in recent weeks, having read far into the night, Eric had risen late. Susan grumbled endlessly about this privilege of his, but Mother steadfastly maintained that he could stay up as late as he wished for a good reason—and reading was a good reason. Lately it seemed to Eric that old difficulties had faded away, only to be replaced by new ones. His parents seemed to understand him better than his friends did. Mother let him stay up half the night reading about snakes, whereas Horse accused him of treachery because he spent time with an old man. Life kept changing, Eric told himself, on the way down to breakfast.

After a few pieces of toast and cool coffee, Eric trudged into the front lawn, watching the fog boil across the grass. Because it was too early for the garden, he decided on taking a little hike. The truth was he had been wanting to take a hike lately, to see other places, but it had seemed disloyal somehow to the garden. This morning, however, he set out through the fog, avoiding the familiar ravines.

He was walking down a street leading to a wooded gully unknown to him, when he saw Silky jogging along the opposite sidewalk. The black kid had a towel slung around his neck. He wore track shorts and a sweat shirt and looked bigger and stronger than he had seemed even a month ago.

Silky waved and crossed the street. "Glad we met," Silky panted. "I was going to phone you. Those guys you're tight with?"

"I'm not tight with any guys," Eric claimed.

"Well, those guys you *were* tight with—they're about to start some real trouble."

"Oh, they talk a lot."

"This time they might be doing more than talk. I heard at Larry's last night they bought some hash from a college dude. They are going to get high and see about your old man."

"Mister Beck?" Eric felt a rush of anger. "They better not touch him."

"Be cool, okay? Cause they are going to see about you, too. That's the word."

"They don't have any reason to get sore."

"No? Seems like you hurt their pride, Eric."

Eric studied the dark face of the runner. Was Silky teasing him? The face said no. But how could he hurt the gang's pride?

"I don't know what you're talking about," Eric said.

"Everybody else does. They said it themselves all over town. How you rather spend time with that old man than them. They didn't even know what they were saying, but they were saying you hurt their feelings. So that's why you better be cool, man."

"When did they say they were going to see about Mister Beck?"

"They didn't say when. I guess when they get high enough on that stuff they got from the college dude, they'll go see about him—and you."

"They talk a lot. They won't hurt anybody," Eric said, trying to reassure himself. But he felt a chill even as he repeated the words: "I've known them a long time; they won't hurt anybody."

"Yeah, well, I hope you're right. But just the same, be cool. I have seen guys like them before. They don't mean anything to start with, but one eggs the other on until they're meaner together than they'd ever be apart. Get my meaning?"

Eric reached out; they slapped palms.

"Later," said Silky and broke into a trot.

Eric turned and watched until the black kid turned the corner. Silky had warned him without saying anything about Mister Beck, without any kind of judgment at all. Silky was okay. As for the gang, they meant nothing to him. He would not believe they could do anything to him, much less to an old man. Maybe he had less respect for their capacity to do harm, because he himself didn't fear them anymore. At least he didn't fear their disapproval. Maybe he still feared them physically, but not the other way, too. He was free of them in his mind.

※　※　※

The fog lifted, and the sun staggered out of a cloud cover by the time he reached the next street. It was going to be a fine day. He took a deep breath, drawing into his nostrils the last moist greenish scent of fog. There was the sun, heating the air, making it throb to the rhythm of summer. And yet summer was fading. Lately he had felt a sense of winding down in the air, a struggle for energy, a lack of ease. Although bright and hot, the sun did not feel right anymore. It lacked that power with which he had watched it climb all summer through the sky, too bright to look at, a great golden disk of flame against the blue backdrop, a glowing furnace of strength, the molten lifeblood of plants in the Beck garden.

In a few more weeks the sun would look different. It would have around it the first haze of autumn; it would take on the kind of thoughtful, hesitant look that men of his father's age wore at the end of the day.

The idea of summer coming to an end was something Eric could not face. He'd rather face Horse or Superkool on a dark street than face the end of summer. It was like the end of summer this year would be the end of everything important. So he wouldn't think about it; he would do something to forget the approach of a new season. Eric came then to a dead-end street beyond which was a gully. He stepped without hesitation into the undergrowth slanting down the hill. He felt a shock wave of cool air, moist from its contact with earth under vegetation. Soon he was enclosed in a green world more familiar to him than the town of streets and houses not a hundred yards away. A few feet farther into the thicket and a low endless drone surrounded him; it was like music, this sound of insects.

Where was he? Near the outskirts of town, maybe a half mile from the Beck place, in one of the countless woods that dotted the hills at the junction of two broad rivers. Eric halted, listening to the chirping of crickets nearby. He dropped to one knee and waited. After a while he separated out from the loud chorus a single bleep, slightly behind his left shoulder. Looking at his watch, he timed the bleeping for exactly fourteen seconds. As well as he could follow the extremely rapid pattern of sound, he counted thirty-four bleeps in that length of time. Adding a constant of forty and recording the time of observation, he wrote the sum down in a little notebook that he had been carrying for weeks. That evening he would call the Weather Bureau and ascertain if the temperature at ten thirteen had been 74 degrees Fahrenheit. Six times this summer he had tried this experiment, and four times the result had been fairly accurate. He hadn't yet explained it to Mister Beck; that would come only when he could report accurate results every time.

Eric went on slowly through the dense woodland. Sugar maples and hickory. Red ash with the underside of their dark leaves fluttering pale and silvery. Lilac milkweeds. Pink clover. Funneled gentians. Leaves moving in tides. The entire tangle of forest bubbling with insects, many of whom, by coloration and shape, tried to outwit his glance; they resembled bird droppings, fungi, the serrated edge of a leaf, a stick, even a flower on its stem.

Prying off some bark from a rotten log, he uncovered an ant colony at work. Big soldiers stood their ground with mandibles chomping the air blindly, while nurses grabbed up the rice-shaped larvae and scuttled for deeper tunnels. For a breathtaking moment Eric watched the immense queen herself, her abdomen swollen like a balloon. He bent close enough to watch an egg pop out of her teeming body like a small expelled seed and a waiting nurse snatch up the white capsule and hurry away. The queen wiggled into a hole, and within moments, down a tunnel her loyal subjects had chewed out of wood, she'd be squeezing out another egg, another, and if she were young, she might still be giving new life to the colony when he, Eric Fischer, was more than thirty years old.

To run off the swarming midges, he swiped at his forehead with the flat of his hand. At a small stream he knelt and watched the incredibly quick water striders and whirligig beetles. Cast skins of flies were strewn all along the eroded bank. Aquatic larvae crawled beneath the clear water along pebbles on the clay bottom. In the trees overhead there were cicadas stridulating. They filled the woods with a languorous drone like air conditioners humming on a hot day.

At last Eric sat down under a tree. Within the dark shade the air was so moist and cool that it felt against his skin like a soft wet veil of the most delicate material. He looked around with the discriminating eye of someone accustomed to looking at nature. This was a good place, even a special place. He calculated offhand that it was about as big as five city blocks. Not so small that you were always in view of houses, but not so big that you were unable to measure it.

And sit in it.

Each six-foot square of it.

This was the sort of place that he and Mister Beck would be requiring soon. Now that the garden was threatened on all sides by the entire town, they would need a new and secret place. They would need it for the autumn when he was not at school and they could sneak away together and work here as they had done in the garden.

It was a satisfying idea, and Eric savored it through long minutes that faded around him like shadows. He rested his chin on his raised knees and gazed contentedly at the undergrowth, the tangle of branches, the swarming air.

There was only one real problem: how to get Mister Beck down the gully.

Eric thought, while flicking at the midges that were forming clouds of irritability near his eyes and nose. Maybe it wouldn't be too hard getting the old man down the hill, not if they used a carefully worked-out plan. For example, Miss Beck could drive the old man to the end of the street; then all they had to do was find a way to transport him down the steep incline of the gully. Maybe use a pulley system. Rig one of those rescue baskets between trees on a large rope and ease him down in it. Not impossible. There must be books on how to rig such a thing. Or maybe Mister Beck still had enough strength left to make it by foot with some help. Say, if a path were cleared through the undergrowth so he wouldn't stumble. And once down into the bottom woods Mister Beck could sit in his chair. They'd bring it down and keep it hidden under some leaves and branches, while the measuring of squares took place. It would be easy to hide almost anything down there when autumn came and the leaves piled up. Mr. Beck could even stay out until it snowed, if they wrapped him in a thick blanket. They might build a little fire. Eric looked around discerningly. A larger garden, that's all. Free of prying eyes, where nobody would think of bothering them, where they wouldn't even have to look at a house or at anything man-made.

Eric stood up and in the full rush of his enthusiasm gave

out a war whoop. And then again. He did it once again, happily aware that nobody would hear him within this dense thicket. Only a few blocks away there were rubber tires slapping heavily on hot cement, but he could not hear them. That was a good omen. Yes, this was the place, their new garden. It wasn't as if they were disloyal to the old one, but until everyone calmed down, it would be better for them to sit here. After all, nothing could ever destroy the first garden; all they could do was add to it.

Eric glanced at his watch: past noon. Too early, in his opinion, to go to the garden and see Mister Beck. Maybe he'd mosey home and get his tape measure and return here long enough to map out the general size and shape of the woods. He'd pace it off rapidly so he could give Mister Beck an initial report.

With that in mind he left the woods, climbing the hillside in a leisurely manner and strolling homeward.

Finally, ahead, he saw the driveway, the clean red brick.

Eric halted in surprise. Running toward him with face flushed and eyes wide and mouth parted was Roddy.

"They're going to get the old man!" Roddy panted, reaching him. "I heard it at the ball park. Some big kids were talking about some other kids getting high and doing it."

"Slow down," said Eric. "Say that again."

"Some kids are going to get high and go after your old man."

Eric stared thoughtfully at his anxious little brother. It couldn't be true. The gang wouldn't do anything really, no matter what Silky and Roddy thought.

"What are you going to *do*?" Roddy asked breathlessly.

He fairly danced up and down in his frustration. "You got to do something! You got to!"

Eric realized with dismay that his little brother's reaction was the right one. There was no time to lose. That old man was sitting unaware of danger in the garden while he himself had taken an aimless hike and put off going there. Because Eric had been denying the danger to himself. Because he had no idea how to handle it.

He turned and was running off.

"Can I go with you?" called Roddy at his back.

Eric glanced over his shoulder at the boy and waved. "Not this time!" And he added, with feeling, "But the next time! Thanks, Roddy! Thanks!"

> ❉ ❉ ❉

He could never recall getting there. He just ran. His heart and mind and body coalesced into one speeding unit, like an arrow, shot toward the garden. He didn't even blame himself for cowardice or inaction; there wasn't time. The ravines and backyards and more ravines became a blur going past his eyes half blinded by the sweat pouring down his face. And then he was in the last ravine and then struggling up the final hill toward the garden, a stitch in his side not even slowing him down, although he clutched the flesh as if to contain the pain until he could reach the top.

He reached it. He burst into the garden, lunging forward so quickly that he almost fell, and to his immense relief Eric saw the old man sitting near the birdbath, mouth open, dozing.

Eric slumped down on the lawn and panted. Rapidly he scanned the whole area, especially the driveway, the neighboring yard. When he had breath enough, Eric trotted to the front lawn and studied the street in both directions: nothing but a solitary woman carrying a bag of groceries. Then he noticed, painted in dripping red letters against the clapboard front of the house, a crude skull and crossbones.

When he returned to the garden, Mister Beck had awakened and was eying him curiously.

"You look like you just fell in the river," Mister Beck said.

"I've been running." Eric glanced suspiciously around. "Where is Miss Beck?"

"Gone to get some paint remover. Seems an amateur artist did a little work on the house."

"Has anybody been around this morning?" Eric trotted over and peered into the dark garage.

"What's got into you, son?"

Eric turned quickly. Son—it was the first time Mister Beck had ever called him that.

"What's the mystery?" Mister Beck asked with a smile.

"Some kids have been around town bragging how they're going to make trouble."

"I see. They want to get the old jailbird. Do you know them, Eric?"

He nodded with a grimace. "They're all right, I guess. Only they don't have much to do, so they think up things like this. And they got some stuff to get high on."

Mister Beck didn't look impressed. He just rearranged the shawl around his thin neck.

"They're not really so bad," observed Eric anxiously, "but the four of them can get worked up."

"Sure. That's the way of the world," said the old man

indifferently. "You take X, Y, and Z separately, and they're docile as lambs. Put them together, they become a roaring lion. Oh, I know that all right."

"Maybe you should go inside the house," Eric suggested timidly.

"Do you think I have lived eighty-two years to be frightened of some bored kids?"

"I wish you'd go inside."

"I will not go inside, but maybe you should."

"Not if you don't."

"I suspect these kids are less interested in hurting me than in scaring you. If you aren't here, they'll leave. So why not go home for the rest of the day?"

"I won't go home. I'm staying with you."

"Go home," Mister Beck said with a frown.

"I won't."

Their eyes met, and this time it was the pair of old blue eyes that wavered and finally looked away. "Then you won't," Mister Beck said with a sigh. "Anyway, I think we're making something out of nothing." He sat back in a relaxed way that reassured Eric, who flopped down beside the chair.

Eric glanced around at the sunlit garden. The garden was sacred.

"I got some news today, Eric, I bet is going to surprise you."

Eric looked up at the old man, who winked at him. Plainly Mister Beck was delighted.

"Remember that art dealer from Chicago? He's going to show my paintings and sell them." Mister Beck chuckled. "That should give the town something to think about."

Eric laughed, too. He was happy for Mister Beck and happy because the town wouldn't know how to accept such news. Now the paroled murderer was an artist! It was funny all right. They were both laughing, looking at each other and laughing, when through the sound they themselves were making, Eric heard something else. It was laughter, too, coming from the direction of the driveway.

Eric leapt to his feet. "They're here."

"Let me handle them," Mister Beck said, clutching the arms of the chair, as if ready for takeoff. "I'll just growl and they'll run."

As the old man made this sardonic remark, two boys appeared around the corner of the house, howling and wearing Spiderman masks.

Spiderman masks. It was a joke! Eric breathed easier and relaxed.

Two other boys emerged from the ravine also wearing the blood-red masks with cobwebby streaks of black.

Howling and leaping, they made a semicircle in front of the chair.

Mister Beck chortled and beat time on the chair arm with the flat of his hand.

Eric couldn't help but smile at the gang's antics: Horse jumped around in a heavy bearish way; Bones hooted like a monkey and wagged his head; Superkool swished along with his hands girlishly on his hips: Zap, the best dancer of the four, was doing a boogie to unseen music. It was like a performance. Eric's heart lifted. Had the gang come to entertain the old man, not to harm him? Eric vowed to apologize if it were true. The gang was okay; their bark was worse than their bite. He had misjudged them, he told himself with conviction, watching Mister Beck pound out the rhythm on the chair.

"Hey! Hey! Hey!" Horse roared suddenly and ripped off his mask. His eyes were half shut, but the dilated pupils seemed bright and feverish. There was a look to them that instantly put Eric on guard. Because Horse was high. Swaying there and grinning, Horse was high. "Look here, mister," he began with a brief chuckle, "it's okay if we come into your garden, isn't it?"

Mister Beck nodded coolly, with a faint smile.

"I mean, you let this cruddy kid"—he turned to glare at Eric—"sit here like a Buddha all the time. So we figure we might come along once, too. Is that okay?"

Mister Beck nodded again.

Horse cocked his head and cupped his ear. "Sorry, mister, but I didn't get your answer."

"It's okay," said Mister Beck.

Zap guffawed; only Horse thus far had removed his mask. The other three stood there looking both ominous and ridiculous. Both, Eric thought. But Horse looked dangerous without the mask, grinning and nasty.

"I'm glad it's okay, mister," he continued, "because we're here and we're going to stay. We got a few questions to ask you. Is that all right with you?"

Mister Beck nodded; his old face remained impassive.

"I'm sorry, mister, but I didn't hear you again."

"It's all right."

"Good, because you see, this cruddy kid here, who was supposed to be our friend, kept sneaking away to see you without ever telling us."

"Did he have to tell you?" Mister Beck asked quietly.

"We tell one another everything," said Horse, hands on hips.

"Do you really do that?"

"Don't get funny with me, old man."

"I'm asking a simple question, *young* man. Do you have a contract drawn up among you that states each of you must tell the others every single thing that happens? Do you?"

Superkool, still wearing a mask, stepped forward and stood beside Horse. "Tell us about the murder, old man."

"Yeah, you tell this cruddy kid here everything. What's wrong with us? Tell us how you killed your wife," said Horse angrily.

"Let him alone!" Eric yelled and took one step forward before being spun aside by Horse, who lunged at the chair and flung it, sprawling Mister Beck onto the lawn along with the pitcher of lemonade and glasses.

Eric didn't think; he just moved. He sprang up and hurtled through the air and grabbed Horse's back. The big guy tossed him off easily, and he felt himself on the ground again. Again he was up, flailing wildly at the masked boy nearest him.

It was Zap who hit him then, full in the face.

The blow leveled Eric, and yet it seemed to clear his head. He got up coldly, deliberately, as if watching himself from a distance. He held his fists out and for a few moments circled around Zap, who did a little dance and invited him "to come on," while the others yelled encouragement.

Eric scarcely heard them. He was into it now, into the physical part of it at last, and so with a kind of relief at knowing it had come, he rushed at Zap and caught the masked boy on the side of the head with a single blow, knocking the mask off and spinning him down. Zap just sat there, legs splayed out, looking stunned at the ground. He didn't say anything; he looked as though he were contemplating blades of grass, sitting there withdrawn and lonely and hurt.

Eric wasted no time turning to the next boy, who was Superkool, whose long blond hair flared around the edges of the mask. Eric waded in with both fists windmilling. The clumsy unmeditated attack seemed to surprise and confuse the stronger boy, because he caught three blows full in the face before delivering one of his own. That single blow hurt Eric, but not as much as he had suspected it would on those numerous occasions when he had regarded Superkool's muscles and wondered how it would feel to be hit by such a strong kid. Now he knew; it hurt, but he was still standing; he was on his feet and still going at Superkool without a pause. His body was doing his thinking, so that even though Eric was small compared to his adversary, each of his blows had his whole strength behind it, making it more punishing than he could believe.

Superkool went down.

Horse yelled scornfully at him to get up and fight.

The fallen boy grabbed Eric's foot, tripping him into the grass. Then they were rolling, first one and then the other on top, their legs twisting for advantage, their arms groping for purchase on arm, neck, chest. They were getting winded, moving slower while Horse taunted them from above. During the tussle Superkool's mask had been ripped off, loosening his long blond hair. He was breathing hard, his eyes glancing wildly around. "Hey, get off," he whimpered. "I can't breathe."

Eric, on top, stared at the flushed face, the fear in those glazed blue eyes.

"I'm too high," panted Superkool. "Get off. I can't breathe—"

Eric rolled off and got to his knees. Facing him were two sturdy legs, the muscles of them taut against jeans. Those legs didn't belong to Bones. Eric felt a sudden rush of fear as he squinted up in the sunlight at the tall thick figure of Horse.

"Come on!" boomed Horse. "Get up!"

Eric could feel the courage leaving him, and yet somehow his legs kept working, kept getting him into an upright position. Just as he straightened up, a blow crashed against his jaw. It felt as if the lower part of his face had fallen off. He was staring at blades of grass, bent and bruised in the struggle, a few inches in front of his nose. A strange sensation was going through his body; it wasn't fear, it was almost pleasant. As if a vacuum were pulling stuff gently out of him.

He was fainting. Yet he blinked rapidly to stay conscious and lifted himself on one elbow.

"That enough?" he heard the big guy say from a great distance above him.

Eric saw the old man sprawled among lemon peels, blue eyes wide open, mouth moving slightly but without sound.

"No," mumbled Eric. The sight of Mister Beck gave him a surge of strength great enough to get him back on his feet. He stood reeling, his fists out.

"You had enough," Horse muttered and turned to walk away.

"Oh, no, he hasn't!" It was Superkool. He had the knife

in his hand, the sheepfoot blade catching a gleam of sunlight, flashing.

"Put that away!" Horse yelled, but the command came late, because Superkool had already thrust with the knife.

Eric felt something like fire in his ribs. He heard his own breath go out in a loud grunt, and then he fell.

He didn't pass out, but heard their excited voices—accusing, complaining. He heard Bones whimpering. He heard Superkool's voice rise into sudden fear: "I didn't mean to! Honest!" And he heard Zap exhorting them to get the hell out of there. And Horse raising his powerful voice in scorn and rage. "You stupid—you—damn you!"

And then Eric heard nothing and saw nothing until again he heard his own breath going out with a kind of whistling moan. He took a deep breath. Pain from it made him scream, and the scream caused more pain. He bit his tongue to keep from crying out again with the next breath he took. Clutching one hand against his side, he felt something sticky between his ribs. Holding up his trembling hand, he saw blood. He was cut badly all right. The sound again—his own moaning. It was like something detached from him, that sound, but the pain was close, intimate; it was deep inside of him just waiting for him to make the slightest move. From where he lay, he could see Mister Beck. Horrified, he was at first sure the old man was dead. Then he saw the lips move, trying to speak. He wanted to help Mister Beck, but the pain wouldn't let him shift one muscle. If he tried to crawl over there to the old man, he'd pass out again.

Their eyes met.

The old blue eyes rolled up again and again as if trying

to tell Eric something. Again and again Mister Beck moved his eyes in a meaningful way.

Then Eric understood. Mister Beck was telling him to look at the sky. Concentrate on it, watch it, until help came. Eric shifted slightly to face the sky. The movement sent a jolt of pain through his rib cage, and he felt himself close to slipping away into unconsciousness. Look up, up, he told himself. There wasn't a cloud to fix on. All he had was a pure blue unmarked slate overhead. Mister Beck was now out of visual range, so Eric was alone with the thing in his side waiting to make him scream. Look at the sky, he told himself. He looked at it until his vision seemed to push farther into its depths, like a diver going down into the deepest sea, until his eyes made him forget the ugly presence of pain, until he was staring clear through the blue sky and meeting a wonderful darkness beyond.

※　※　※

Concussion. A broken jaw. Cuts and bruises. Punctured lung. Severe bleeding. Almost didn't make it. But the deepest, most painful wound remained in his mind and would not heal. As Eric lay in the hospital bed and watched people march in to see him, he hated them all. They had all done it, the townspeople, they had all put him into this bed and Mister Beck into one down the hall. The gang had only been their infantry, their foot troops; that's all. He understood after a while that the gang hadn't meant to do anything. They had got high and put on some stupid masks for a lark, not really dead set on hurting him or the old man. But when they got there and failed to rouse any reaction of fear in him or in Mister Beck, they became confused and didn't know what to do. So they struck out. It was what people did when they worked together in a group without knowing exactly why they were together.

All this was explained to him by his parents, who came every day and sat with him.

At first he viewed them, too, with contempt and suspicion. And then he softened in the face of their sympathy and anxiety for him. And for Mister Beck, too. Every day Mother brought him a report on Mister Beck's condition. He'd had a mild stroke, but the prognosis was excellent. She had even met him.

"What do you think?" Eric asked shyly.

Mother seemed embarrassed by the question. After all, it wasn't every day that her son asked her to comment on a convicted murderer.

"He seems very nice to me," Mother finally said.

Eric would not be satisfied with such a bland answer. "Tell me," he urged.

"Very well. We had a little talk. He told me never in his life had anyone fought for him except two people. His daughter and you. His left arm is crippled and his speech is impaired, but, Eric, when he mentioned your name, I don't think I have ever seen a man look happier. Now is that what you want to know?" she added with a smile.

"I'll see him again when I get out of here."

Mother sighed. "I guess you will. I guess nobody will stop you from doing that. And he'll probably be in the garden waiting. He gets out before you do. The doctors say he's a medical marvel. Do you want to be wheeled down there to see him?"

Eric shook his head. "When we meet, it's got to be in the garden."

After that conversation with Mother, he began to feel better; the wound in his mind began to heal, and he could smile at people who came to visit him, even at Sally Wilson, who came with a group of admiring girls and who never smiled back but continued to stare at him in that disconcerting way. A lot of kids from school came, for he had become something of a celebrity. Even Roddy gave him a long glance of respect for having stood up to four guys like that, and one of them as big as Horse and the other as dangerous as Superkool. It was strange how a town acted, Eric thought. Attention had shifted from the old murderer to the young tough—which is what some people called Superkool. Opinion came down heavily on him, and the same people who had called for running the Becks out of town were disappointed that the boy got only six months in the state reformatory; they were furious that the other boys only got lengthy probations. That was how a town behaved, Eric thought, and even though he began to feel better about life, he'd never put his trust in a town's ability to sift out the truth from gossip, the right from wrong. When he thought about the gang, he remembered what Father had said while sitting on the hospital bed in the second week of his recuperation.

Father had said, "Anybody can commit one senseless impulsive act that changes his whole life. That's what those kids did. Especially the boy who stabbed you. One moment —his whole life to regret it."

Eric had liked that, because it was the truth, because it had happened exactly that way to Mister Beck.

❧ ❧ ❧

After ten days at home, his ribs still felt sore and the wiring hadn't been removed from his jaw yet, but the pain was almost gone. And he couldn't wait any longer. In spite of family protests, he got himself downstairs and insisted on waiting until they had all gone about their own pursuits before getting himself outside. He was wobbly but determined and waved at his freckled next-door neighbor who waggled her drink at him and called out, "Good to have you back, Eric old boy! That drink's waiting for you any time you want it!"

He could have phoned Mister Beck first to say he was coming, but they had never once used the phone in the past, so it wouldn't be the right way now. He'd just show up in the garden. And as usual he'd get there through the back ravines even if walking up and down those steep inclines became painful. Because it was the way he must get there.

And so, slowly through the morning sunlight, he got himself up one gully and down the next, going on until none of it mattered—the town, the attack, the pain, the hatred—nothing mattered except the last slope that he must climb to get to the garden. The effort gave him a few sharp twinges in the lung, but not enough to dull the pleasure of his anticipation, for he could picture in his mind everything being in place—tree, flower bed, birdbath, Mister Beck in the chair—as he trudged up through the sumac and weeds.

And in fact, when finally he emerged onto the lawn of the garden, nothing had changed. Not even Mister Beck, who sat as usual in a chair—though now a wheelchair—near the birdbath. The old man was taking a nap, his head resting on his sunken chest, his hands hanging over the arms of the chair. Eric hunkered down at the edge of the garden, not wishing to wake his friend for a while. It was enough to look at the garden that he had missed desperately for three weeks. What he must do now, however, was stay away from it as much as possible.

He had worked on this idea while lying in the hospital bed.

He'd explain the plan to Mister Beck. What they must do, they must chart that dense woodland just as they had done the garden. On the morning of the attack he had seen it and loved it, and through long hours in the hospital he had imagined the two of them making this new country their own just as they had made the garden theirs. He'd concentrate hard in every inch of it until it was his and Mister Beck's. The sitting might take a long time, possibly a year, before this tangled forest became theirs. He'd have to go out alone when it got cold. He'd crouch in the snow for hours, making the land theirs, until the cold clung to the marrow of every bone in his body. He'd have to acquaint himself with the woods in every season to get the feel of each change. He'd have to watch the trees carefully, how their silhouettes changed when the leaves fell and the branches were bare, and how they took a different shape when the budding began next spring. And then there was the stream. He had to fix that for them in his mind, too, and it wouldn't be easy, because the stream had life on its surface and life on its bottom and life under its twisting banks, and he'd have to watch what happened when ice began to edge along its sides and finally held it solid except for a thin line of water trickling through a small channel like blood in a tiny vein. He thought so hard of the woodland in wintertime that he could almost shiver. It would be difficult to make that country theirs, but he could do it alone in winter, and then in spring, when Mister Beck could join him again, they'd do it together.

Then Eric blinked and focused on the garden, aware that his T-shirt was soaked through with sweat. He glanced up, noticing a small V of ducks overhead, navigating south for the winter.

He glanced then apprehensively at Mister Beck, who was still napping in the wheelchair. Eric sighed; everything was okay. He'd wake the old man now and explain the new plan. His only regret was his inability to carry the old man on his back into the woods. For that they would have to rig up a rescue chair.

"Here I am," he said, putting his hand gently on Mister Beck's shoulder. The old man didn't stir. Eric shook him a little harder, without result. He knelt and studied the sunken head. The blue eyes were open, staring wide without blinking. They were like marbles.

Eric, letting out a short cry, touched the old gnarled hand —it was cold. He touched the other one; it, too, was cold. Then he lifted Mister Beck's arm, as if trying to get it started, like cranking an old car. Such a weightless, shriveled arm. Nothing to it at all. He began to pat the old man gently on the back, as if to comfort him, looking through tears not at the hunched slumping body but at the garden under sunlight.

Then helplessly Eric flung himself down at the old man's feet. He stared numbly at the big shoes sticking out from under the shapeless pants.

It wasn't fair. They hadn't had a last word together. He had always figured that at the last—when their summer was over—they'd have time to say a few things. And he hadn't even been able to tell Mister Beck about the woods they would see together. Mister Beck would have liked that, and there hadn't been time.

It wasn't fair.

Eric looked desperately in the direction of the house. Perhaps Miss Beck was home. Then he glanced dismally at the big black shoes, a little film of dust over the toes. One of the laces, having been broken a few times, had knots in it. Miss Beck was fastidious, so it must have been that Mister Beck wouldn't let her touch his things; he had lived forty years alone in a cell, and in his last days he wouldn't let a woman, not even his daughter, fuss over him.

The socks emerging from the shoes were black, too, fallen slackly around the ankles, because the old man lacked flesh enough to keep them up.

It wasn't fair. Not even one last word.

"Oh, Mister Beck," Eric whispered, getting to his feet and forcing himself to look at the bald head sunken against the chest. "Oh, Mister Beck," he said at the sky.

Then clearing his throat he called for the daughter, at first timidly, then in a loud firm voice.

Soon he heard her answer from the kitchen window. She wanted to know what was wrong. But Eric didn't have to tell her, because she could see through the screen, and the next moment she was coming out of the house, murmuring something under her breath that sounded to him like no, no, a kind of keening sound and yet a sound without surprise, as if she had been preparing for this moment a long time.

Eric backed away from the chair and let her come to it

alone; the gaunt, gray-haired woman fell to her knees and grasped the old limp hand and held it to her cheek, saying something gently, her eyes filling with tears.

It was time for him to go, Eric knew. Miss Beck and her father had never had much real time together, only brief visits through a wire screen each month at the prison. They deserved these last moments alone.

But Eric didn't want to go. This is where he belonged, here in the garden with Mister Beck.

He stared at the woman, who seemed to have forgotten him, and in those moments he realized that father and daughter had become united in her grief, because in spite of everything she had managed all those years to love her father, and now, here in the garden, she was saying good-bye.

Eric had to go. It was their time, not his. And yet he understood that if he left the garden now, he would never see it again. He glanced in every direction at flower, tree, lawn. He had to say good-bye right now, this moment.

Eric wiped his nose on the back of his hand and turned for the ravine. He had to let the garden go and keep it another way. Through his tears he squinted at the rectangle of sky directly overhead and watched a cloud hovering over the garden. He felt the terrible pain of loss, worse than the pain in his lung had ever been. He felt something going out of him. Was it Mister Beck? The garden? It was both. And yet they would be with him, inside of him, wherever he went from this moment on.

Eric took his first step into the ravine. He did not look back.

ABOUT THE AUTHOR

Malcolm J. Bosse teaches in the Department of English at The City College of New York. Currently he is teaching and lecturing on a Fulbright-Hays Grant in India. He has received many awards for his writing, including the Masefield Award for Poetry from Yale University and two major Hopwood Awards for poetry and fiction from the University of Michigan. Among his publications are three novels and several short stories for adults. The 79 Squares *is his first novel for young adults. His many varied interests extend to Tai Chi Chuan, oriental mythology, jazz, sculpture, and myrmecology (study of ants). Mr. Bosse lives with his wife and son in New York City.*